Loyal Judas

"What If ... Biblical fiction" series, Volume 1

Lila Diller

Published by Lila Diller, 2022.

LOYAL JUDAS

First edition. April 1, 2022.

Copyright © 2022 Lila Diller.

ISBN: 979-8201062347

Written by Lila Diller.

DEDICATION:

We would like to dedicate this book to our spiritual mentor, Greg Boyd. His work on open theism and free will has totally changed our perspectives and freed our minds from the slavery of legalistic determinism. His books (especially *Benefit of the Doubt*) were pivotal during a time of Chris's crisis of faith.

Thank you, Greg, for both being our virtual pastor and our theological shepherd. Keep up the good work of wrestling with the hard things and sharing them with us!

AUTHORS' NOTE: PLEASE READ FIRST!

This is a work of fiction. Though based off the New Testament, it's merely a figment of our imaginations.

Please don't consider anything in this book as inspired or replacing the Bible in any way. While we have tried to remain as true to the Gospels as possible up until after the Last Supper, we make no bones about departing from the Scripture after that.

Judas betrayed Jesus and then hung himself. But we really don't know much about him other than that.

This book is an imaginative answer to the question, "What if?" What if Judas had made a different choice? Consider it **speculative** Biblical fiction.

Our hope is that though the real Judas did *not* choose to repent and follow Jesus in real life, **you can**. Anyone can be redeemed. Jesus is powerful enough and gracious enough to redeem even the worst of sinners.

Even me. Even you.

TABLE OF CONTENTS

CHAPTER 1 THE CALLING

I was minding my own business. Really. I didn't plan to get involved. I almost didn't. I wonder how my life would have turned out?

I was waiting in line at Levi's tax booth, waiting to ask for yet another extension on the payment deadline for my father's taxes.

Father always means well, but the call of the market, with all its bustle, wares, and salesmen, always tempts him to throw away his good intentions.

I don't know how many times I've been left to pick up the slack. I was so sick and tired of feeling humiliated while trying to clean up his messes.

Like I said, I was just minding my own business in line, when a group of men walked up the road. A dusty man in the front was obviously the leader, for though he didn't call attention to himself, all of his followers fawned over every word he said.

I watched as he held up his hand for his entourage to stop. He and three of his main groupies walked right on past those of us in line and close to Levi.

I grumbled, "Doesn't he know there's a line? We were here first."

Not that I was eager for the interview. But it was my right to be rewarded for my patience in line.

I think one of his followers heard me, for he looked over and sniffed his disgust.

"Shows what you know. Don't you know who that is?"

His remark didn't even deserve a reply. Instead, I scowled to cover my ignorance.

He continued, "That's Jesus of Nazareth!"

My eyes opened wide, seemingly of their own volition. Oh, so that was Jesus of Nazareth, the prophet everybody was whispering about.

Jesus called out to Levi, "Follow me." Levi had a strange expression on his face. I had never seen him look humbled and yet happy.

I heard Levi say in a contrite tone, "I wish to follow you, but I've done some cruel things. How can you accept me?"

Jesus paused for a dramatic moment and looked him directly in the eyes. "Your name is now Matthew. You are a new person. You will no longer steal and cheat. Forget about the past. You will be greatly used in my Father's kingdom."

Levi's smile was like nothing I had ever seen before. I envied his feeling of acceptance. My father had never made me feel accepted. Never would.

Why should Levi get special treatment? What made him any better than me?

I grumbled to the old man in front of me. "Who does he think he is?"

I thought I was quiet enough that Jesus wouldn't hear me. I was wrong.

He turned and gazed straight into my soul. I felt so exposed. But Jesus remained silent for several minutes. Was he angry with me? What would he do?

Finally, after sweat beads began to form on my forehead, Jesus' eyes softened and he held out his hand. "Come and follow me."

Seriously? He heard me complaining about his superiority complex and he still wanted me to be one of his followers?

Surely that's not what he meant. Maybe he just wanted me to follow him for the afternoon and watch an object lesson or something.

What could it hurt? I still needed to talk to Levi and hopefully use this situation to get out of debt.

I nodded and fell into step behind Jesus and Levi. I tried to ignore the looks his loyal three were shooting at me and Levi. And the one guy who had talked to me made sure to stay as far away from me as possible. His fine robes told me he thought I was poor and beneath him. I'll bet he was out to get some power by being associated with Jesus, too.

Oh, maybe that's why Levi had followed Jesus. Maybe Jesus had offered him a higher paying job when he overthrew the Romans and became king of Judea.

That sounded like a better gig than I could ever hope for. Assistant at my father's woven goods booth at the market payed very little. And with my father's reputation, there was no opportunity for anything else.

Maybe I would follow this Jesus for a while longer, if he really wanted me. I didn't see why he would, but maybe he was looking for hard luck cases. In that case, I was his man.

CHAPTER 2 THE WEDDING

Those first few months, though I went home to help my father a couple of days a week, I made it my main job to observe everything I could about the Master. I listened to the disciples that had begun following him first, Andrew and the fishermen.

They told us the stories of how they had spent an entire night of catching nothing. Jesus had told them to let their nets down one more time, and they did, and miraculously they had caught more fish than their nets could hold.

Instead of selling this surplus, they left everything and followed him. I could see that Levi might be promised a high position and a great-paying job once Jesus overthrew the Romans. But what in the world could fishermen hope to gain more than fish?

I listened as they told about meeting Jesus' family at the wedding in Cana. I heard how his mother Mary expected him to do something about the wine shortage.

I doubted very much that the disciples had been sober enough to realize what was really going on, so they made up a an entertaining but untrue story about Jesus turning vats of water into good wine.

But believe me, I heard about it so much I was sick of hearing about "water into wine."

The other disciples believed he performed a miracle that day. I don't know how he did it, but that doesn't mean it had to be a supernatural act of God through this prophet-like, Messiah-claimer.

Maybe he was just a good trickster, a charismatic illusionist, a street magician. He didn't seem to draw attention to himself on purpose, though.

It was just natural for people to want to see his signs and tricks. He did them like it was natural for him, with no fanfare, other than an occasional, informal prayer to Adonai.

I also heard that though it was obvious his mother believed he was a messenger from Adonai, his brothers seemed to scoff. They were probably jealous.

It reminded me of the story of one of our most favorite patriarchs, Joseph, son of Isaac, son of Abraham. His brothers had been so jealous that they sold him into slavery.

I hoped that Jesus' brothers wouldn't think to try anything like that, or I would be in major trouble. I couldn't afford anything other than enough funds to purchase my plot of land.

It would be mine.

CHAPTER 3 THE CHOSEN

It had been a few weeks. We followed Jesus of Nazareth around everywhere and listened to him teach. One morning just after dawn, Jesus called together all of us disciples.

"You have all followed me from the beginning of my ministry. Now I need twelve of you to be my apostles, my closest advisers and friends. You twelve will be the chosen leaders once I'm gone. You will continue to spread the Good News."

I had no idea what Good News he was talking about. So far, the only good news I had seen was Jesus' miraculous ability to heal any and all diseases, like that man who had a deformed right hand and was healed on the Sabbath day last week.

Boy were those Pharisees hopping mad! Jesus really did break the laws of the Talmud when he healed on the holy day of the Sabbath. But Jesus didn't care. He had just looked at each of them with that soul-scraping stare of his and used what I would come to find as one of his favorite teaching tools—asking more questions.

"I have a question for you. Does the law permit good deeds on the Sabbath, or is it a day for doing evil? Is this a day to save life or to destroy it?"

Of course, no one would answer. But everyone knew it was right to do good, even on the Sabbath. I had never thought about it before.

But how would angering the Pharisees be Good News worth spreading? And what did he mean now by saying, "Once I'm gone"? Where would he go?

Maybe he planned to set up his Messiah-ruled kingdom and then go off to conquer other lands. Or maybe he planned to retire and let us rule everything. That would work. As long as I could be one of the twelve.

I knew I stood a good chance, because he had personally invited me to follow him. He didn't do that for most of his followers. Many were just groupies, following the latest rising superstar.

But then he began to solemnly name and point to the special twelve.

"Simon. You will be called Peter, the pebble. And your brother Andrew. James and John, you sons of Zebedee. Philip, Bartholomew. Matthew, no more will you be called Levi."

I was slightly surprised that Levi made it. After all, he had been a tax collector, a greedy, cruel, no-good thief. But then, Jesus had specifically invited him, too. Of course, he wouldn't leave him behind. But why did he give him and Simon new names?

"Thomas." Ah, the first guy who had spoken to me, the one who had been disgusted with me.

"James, son of Alphaeus." Another James? Boy, this might get confusing.

"Simon." He pointed at a good-looking man I had found out had been a member of the zealots, also trying to overthrow Rome. Surely, that proved that Simon the zealot at least thought that Jesus was the best chance to take down those profane Roman Gentiles.

When he said, "Judas," my heart skipped a beat, but Jesus pointed at the other Judas, the son of yet another James. I sighed. What was I thinking? I had no skills to be used in the new kingdom. I didn't know how to fight like Simon the zealot. I did know how to handle money, but Levi, I mean Matthew, was likely much better at that than me.

But then again, why did he choose the fishermen? And why the boyish James son of Alphaeus? Maybe he had some other qualifications he was looking for.

How many had that been? Was that the last one, or was there one more?

I quickly counted the ones Jesus had already pointed out, who had made their way to the front. Eleven. That was only eleven. There would be one more. My last chance.

Jesus was sure taking his time choosing this last one. The tension was killing me. I couldn't go back. I just couldn't go back to my father and tell him I hadn't been chosen, that I was a loser yet again.

Please, Jesus, I silently begged. Please pick me. I knew it was superstitious. Not like he could hear me. But I thought it wouldn't hurt to try to influence my luck.

Then Jesus swiveled around and stared straight at me. I held my breath. Could it be possible?

Jesus' smile didn't reach his eyes, but he pointed right at me. "Judas Iscariot."

I let out my breath. I smiled at Jesus and then took my place next to the other eleven. I was one of the chosen ones. Finally, something in my life was going right.

Thomas and Matthew gave me sidelong glances, the hostility from Thomas far outweighing the mere interest from Matthew. I was going to need to watch my back with Thomas. He might try to change Jesus' mind.

Jesus allowed us to quickly say goodbye to our families.

I almost decided to leave without saying any goodbyes, but the other disciples would have looked at me funny if I hadn't left when Levi had.

So I ran back home to say goodbye to the little hut that had been my home all my life. Father was snoring in his room, the smell of the empty bottles mixing with unpleasant body odors.

I didn't want to wake him to tell him what he would probably see as bad news, but I didn't have time to wait for him to wake up on his own.

I shook him until he finally opened his eyes. "Father? I'm leaving. I don't know how long I'll be."

"What? Where you going, Boy?"

I pursed my lips. Couldn't Father tell I wasn't a boy anymore? My beard had been full for a while now. Several years at least.

"I've been chosen to be a follower of Jesus of Nazareth."

"Jesus? That so-called prophet? Can anything good come from Nazareth?" His mumbled words were slurred and sluggish as he fought a hangover.

I sighed. I didn't have time for this.

"Yes, Father. He is a prophet of Adonai, I think. He's been performing miracle after miracle. And he specifically asked me to follow him. So I'll be going with him for a while. I don't know how long. Maybe months."

"Months? What am I going to do without you for so long?"

I laughed in his face. "You're always saying I'm a no-good lazy bum. Now you'll get to see how much I actually do around here. Goodbye, Father."

I turned and walked out. I never looked back, even when I heard Father calling my name at the door.

CHAPTER 4 THE MOUNT

Jesus then led us chosen twelve, as well as the other groupie disciples, up to one of the hills overlooking the Sea of Galilee. He bade us to sit down and listen.

As Jesus taught, I was struck with the differences between his teaching and the scribes and Pharisees' recitations. Jesus used simple, easy-to-understand words but delved into deep subjects right from the start.

I loved the rhythm of his words, spoken like any good oral teacher wanting his students to be able to remember his words.

"Blessed are the poor in spirit, the humble, because the kingdom of heaven is theirs. Blessed are they who mourn, because they will be comforted. Blessed are the gentle, because they're going to inherit the earth. Blessed are those who hunger and thirst for righteousness, desiring to live godly lives, because they will be filled up. Blessed are the compassionate, because they will be given compassion. Blessed are those with pure hearts, because they will experience God. Blessed are lovers of peace, because they will be called the children of God."

I wondered how blessed the poor and hungry and meek could really be. Was it just a feeling, an illusion of blessedness? I thought blessings were things I could touch and own, like land, animals, and money. That's what the patriarchs had been "blessed" with in the Pentateuch. Would the poor be blessed with money? I liked that idea. My father and I sure needed more "blessings."

When Jesus continued these blessings, he said something that really rocked my world.

"Blessed are those who are persecuted because of their righteousness, because theirs is the kingdom of heaven. And blessed are you when others taunt you and persecute you and speak all kinds of evil things against you, lying about you because of me. Rejoice and be thankful for this grace, then, because your reward will be great in heaven. In the same way, they persecuted the prophets who came before you. You're in good company."

Then Jesus talked about loving your enemies. I saw Matthew nodding along, like he understood exactly what Jesus was saying. How in the world can anyone really feel love for their enemy? Isn't love a fond feeling? It's not possible to make yourself feel fond of an enemy. So what was Jesus trying to say? That we're expected to do the impossible? Then what was the point of the Law then?

I just felt more and more confused.

Did that mean I had to "love" the Romans who seized my mother away from me as a boy?

My mind took me back to that day. The day my world changed.

As an only child, I helped both my father and mother. When my father took business trips, I was the man of the house.

That day Father was coming home from a long trip. Mother and I took turns looking out the window for him.

I helped mother stoke the fire and brought more water from the river. We tried to find chores to keep us busy until Father returned. We washed the bedding and hung them out on the line to dry behind the house.

Then I heard them, the clod of many soldiers' feet. I ran to the front yard hoping to see Father.

I stopped short when I saw the half-dozen soldiers marching up to our door. I watched wide-eyed, heart pounding, time slowing, as the captain nodded to two of the soldiers to enter.

I heard my mother's voice first asking a question, then her volume raised and the tone sounded hysterical.

My feet were rooted to the ground. Paralyzed, I gasped as the soldiers came out of our house, one on each side of my mother, holding her wrists with the heavy chains of Roman prisoners.

She was struggling, yelling, "Let go! Let go! I've done nothing wrong! Don't take me from my son! Adonai, help!"

Finally, my feet could move, and I ran in front of the soldiers. "Stop! You can't take her!"

One soldier looked somewhat sympathetic but then schooled his expression into blankness. The other scoffed and pushed me out of the way with one armored, muscled arm. I grabbed onto it and tried to pull him the opposite way.

"No! No! I'll do anything! What do you want with her?"

No one answered. I didn't rate an answer. I pulled and tried to kick his legs but to no avail. I was a scrawny little eight-year-old. I stood no chance against a battle-hardened warrior.

He eventually shook me off his arm and pushed me into the mud. I scrambled to get up and protect Mother, but it was too late. They were already halfway down the road, and two of the soldiers had been left behind to make sure I didn't follow. I zigzagged through them, but they caught me before I could reach Mother.

The last words I ever heard her speak were, "Judas, I love you! Take care of your father!"

The soldiers held me until I had struggled all I could. Exhausted, I finally went limp and began to weep. When they were sure I was broken enough to stay, they left without a word. No explanation.

Father came home an hour or two later. I didn't know how much time had passed, only that it felt like an eternity alone and that the sun was low in the west.

When Father saw me laying in the mud, he quickly dismounted and ran to me. "What happened, Judas? Are you all right?"

I couldn't answer. I had thought I was all cried out, but my throat was still clogged and burning.

He grabbed my arms and in fear gave me a little shake. "Judas, answer me! What happened?"

I choked out, "They took her. Mother." I could go no further and sobbed even more.

Father's eyes widened. He let me go and jumped up, running into the house calling, "Rachel! Rachel! Where are you? Rachel!"

He ran all the way around our property calling her name. When he made his way back to me, he picked me up, fear making him rough.

"Judas! Where is she? Who took her? Where?"

"Soldiers. Romans. I don't know where or why."

"The Romans?" His eyes were stricken. His face went white. Father slumped to the ground in a heap and began sobbing, too. "No, no, no! Why her? It's not fair!"

Finally he stopped. The sun had set now, and the chill of the autumn dusk made me shiver.

When Father's sobs subsided, I sat down beside him and wrapped my arms around him as far as they would go.

"It's all right, Father," I comforted. "We'll get her back. We'll find her. I know we will. She prayed to Adonai to help her. We'll be Adonai's tools to help her."

Father pulled away from my embrace and coldly said, "No, Judas. We can't get her back. There's no way we can pay the taxes we owed. She's their slave now, working in exchange for our debt. Adonai won't ever help her. Adonai won't help us, either. He doesn't care."

My broken heart splintered into a thousand pieces. Father wouldn't help her. Adonai wouldn't help her. Mother was helpless.

I didn't let Father see me cry anymore, but I cried myself to sleep every night for almost a month before I toughened up.

I had tried a few times to comfort Father or to share memories of Mother, but he always pulled away or interrupted me. He refused to talk about her or the debt situation.

When I was old enough to start helping keep records, I found out how much our debt had been. Father was right. There was no way we could have ever paid it off to free Mother.

What he didn't tell me was that the debt had been all his fault, from his drinking, gambling, and foolish investments. He tried to ignore the guilt by taking it out on me.

From that day on, my life was misery. I missed Mother, avoided Father as much as possible, and pleased him as best as I could when I had to be around him.

Leaving him to follow Jesus had been easy. Hearing I needed to forgive and love the Romans who had forced my mother away, as well as the father who was to blame, was another story. If Jesus thought a sermon was going to change my mind, he was a fool.

Jesus' eloquent yet simple sermon waxed long. He took a break for refreshments. I didn't see where the bread and water came from that day.

He then bounced around to several different themes: being salt and light, divorce, anger, lust, taking oaths. I didn't know what to make of Jesus. He taught radical things. He made it sound like the Law didn't even go far enough; that just lusting for a woman was already committing adultery and just being angry with a brother was already committing murder. I didn't understand.

The last topic of the day really sent me into a mental spiral.

Jesus ended with a parable about building on a rock or building on sand.

"But anyone who hears and doesn't obey is like a person who builds a house without a foundation. When the floods sweep down against that house, it will collapse into a heap of ruins."

He looked right at me. He seemed to be warning me that I was one of the people building on the sand. Why? What had I done? I had obeyed his call so far.

What else did he want from me? Did he really expect me to love my enemies, never lust, never get angry, never use an oath? That wasn't very fair. What about the other apostles? Why didn't he pick on them?

When we left the mount of his first sermon, I had more questions than answers.

CHAPTER 5 THE COST

I saw Jesus' popularity with the common people. He always had flocks of people following him, like a good shepherd. I knew that if he kept gaining popularity and didn't rock the boat too much with the religious leaders, we would see him as the next ruler of Israel.

I often fantasized about Jesus as king and me as his second-in-command. My exact duties in this new political system were always hazy, but they were always perfectly aligned with my talents and desires.

Of course, I would own any property I wanted. And my name would finally no longer be associated with my Father. My reputation would be connected with the new king instead.

When Jesus began teaching about the cost of being a disciple, I paused. I pulled back from the passion I saw in the eleven.

When Jesus spoke of leaving father and mother, I thought, I've already done that. Mother was taken from us, and father is finally reaping the consequences of his laziness. But I will be rewarded for my sacrifices. At least, I'd better be!

When he spoke of hating them in respect to how we should love God, I dismissed it as rhetoric. He was just feeding the crowd sentimental jargon to stoke their political passions.

When He spoke of persecutions and carrying the cross, though, I panicked. What have I gotten myself into?

When Jesus began speaking about the dichotomy of losing your life to save it and being last to be first, I inwardly scoffed. That's contradictory to all human experience. It can't really work that way. It can't be what he really meant.

"No servant can serve two masters, for either he will hate the one and love the other, or he will be devoted to the one and despise the other. You cannot serve God and money."

Jesus glanced my way again.

Then I began to debate within myself. Can't I serve God and be prosperous, too? Can't I serve God and be rich, like the Pharisees? Can't I serve God and not worry about a roof over my head or where my next meal is going to come from? I've lived with that weight pressing down on me my whole life. I've never known the peace of mind of having enough. Isn't it my turn? Don't I deserve a little reward for serving God?

Jesus glanced my way and shook his head ever so slightly. Nobody else even caught it. But I knew he meant it in response to my thoughts. How did he know what I was thinking?

My first inkling that something was really wrong was when Jesus' most staunch supporter, his cousin John the Baptist, sent a message to Jesus while imprisoned in Herod's dungeon.

Andrew had known many of John's followers, for he had been one. His brother Peter, with his loud mouth, made sure he announced each one by name so we all knew he knew what he was talking about. For once.

John's disciples asked, "Are you the one who is to come, or should we look for another?"

Jesus looked sad but answered them, "Go and tell John what you hear and see: the blind receive their sight and the lame walk, lepers are cleansed and the deaf hear, and the dead are raised up, and the poor have good news preached to them. And blessed is the one who is not offended by me."

But he didn't actually answer the question. Yes, the Messiah was prophesied to do all those things. But so have many of the prophets in generations past.

As far as encouragement goes, that message would not have given me peace in my dying hours.

And it was John the Baptist's dying hours.

We got word a few days later that Herod's wife had connived to get John's head on a platter. His disciples were all mourning, but Jesus took the news in stride. Like he wasn't surprised.

I guess none of us, knowing about Herod's cruelty, should have been surprised. But Herod seemed to like listening to John's preaching. Even if he never changed any of his ways, he still listened and respected John.

But that wife of his. She had always hated John, from the first time he had rebuked her for her adultery. I guess she didn't like her promiscuous little toes being stepped on. Even by a man of God.

Those *ethnōn*, those "other people," are all the same. Heathen reprobates. And the Jews helping them, like the tax collectors and Roman yes-men? I could spit in their faces if I wasn't afraid of getting myself killed or even further into debt.

Jesus seemed to care about everyone, not just us Jews, though he did say his ministry was to the Jews. He even told that Canaanite woman that the dogs, the non-Jews, don't get the main meal, but then he went ahead and still healed her daughter of those demons.

But when his own cousin was imprisoned, he did nothing. He didn't even mourn his death with the usual wailing. He did seem a little heavier than usual, and he withdrew to a solitary place, up on the mountain where he often went by the Sea of Galilee.

That was all the Baptist got. What a reward. What a cost!

CHAPTER 6 THE TRIP

Very early in our ministry, Jesus sent us twelve disciples out to do street ministry. We were supposed to go to a town we'd never been to and begin preaching "the kingdom message."

I had no problem proclaiming that the new Messiah's kingdom was coming soon. My passion for a place in this new kingdom gave me plenty of motivation to get dusty and tired with no preparation whatsoever.

The first thing I would do in this new kingdom would be to set up organization for our group.

For now, I chose to go to Ptolemais a town closer to Cilicia than I normally would like. And it wasn't mainly Jewish, like Jesus wanted us to stick to. But it was on the coast. I had always wanted to see the coast with my parents when I was young.

But I had also heard that this port city was very generous and liked to help the poor. I was sure I could persuade them to line my money bag.

I mean, it was technically Jesus' money bag. But I was in charge of knowing how much we had to spend and getting the best deals. The more donations I could score, the better our lives.

Though Ptolemais was more than 40 miles from Capernaum, our base, I took the opportunity to catch a ride with a caravan of traders. All I had to do was promise to entertain them every night with stories, once they heard I was part of Jesus of Nazareth's entourage. They had heard many rumors about him and wanted me to set them straight. I did.

As I was preaching through the town that first day, I noticed a lot of Roman soldiers. I didn't know if I would have any trouble with them. As long as I wasn't stirring up an actual rebellion or keeping people from their work for too long, I should be okay.

When I stopped talking to go to the well and ask for a drink, I noticed a woman with graying hair and expensive clothing. Maybe I could ask her for a donation as well as a drink.

I approached her with my hands out, palms up, in the usual non-threatening stance. "Excuse me, ma'am, would you mind getting me a drink of water? I'm a stranger in your town."

She sized me up with her dark eyes, the crows' feet around her eyes smoothing out a bit as she determined I was a man of integrity where women are concerned.

My mind flashed back to when my mother had told me that women, though under the authority of men, were special gifts from God.

I remembered her smile as she patted my shoulder. "Remember that though women are the weaker vessel in physical strength, we are the moral strength of Israel. Treat us with respect, and you will be a good man, Judas."

The woman in front of me smiled and answered, "Of course, sir. Strangers are taken care of here."

That smile looked so familiar. As she bent down to scoop the water into her jug, I saw the scars on the back of her wrists, like that of a prisoner held by Roman chains. The memory of mother's fight to return to me and the chains clasped onto her wrists invaded my mind and quickened my heartbeat.

It couldn't be. "Mother?"

She whipped around, water dripping out of the jug. Without taking her eyes off mine, she fumbled to set the jug down on the side of the stone well.

I met her halfway, and she reached up to touch my cheek. Tears welled up in those dark eyes as she choked out, "Is that you, Judas?"

My throat clogged up. I couldn't speak. I nodded and grabbed her hand.

She smiled and tightened her grip on my hand. "What a handsome man you've grown to be!"

Though my heart was full, my mind was blank. What could I say to this now strange woman who missed two thirds of my life?

She asked, "What are you doing here in Ptolemais?"

I cleared my throat and searched for the right words. "I'm an itinerant preacher right now, spreading the news that the kingdom is at hand for Jesus of Nazareth."

Cold began to settle my stomach. What if she thought I was crazy or lazy? I still cared what she thought.

Her eyes widened, almost eliminating the crows' feet. Sadly, I thought that I had missed the coming of her wrinkles and streaks of gray hair. I wondered if I could have saved her some of the stress and worry that must have brought them on.

"Jesus of Nazareth? The Prophet of Adonai? How wonderful, Judas! You are being used by the Lord Himself!"

Her smile radiated from her eyes and lit up the entire square. The cold began to dissipate in my stomach.

"Oh, your drink! If you've been traveling and preaching, your throat must be dry. Here you go, Son."

Son. How my ears loved to hear that word from her lips!

As I drank, I contemplated how the name Son sounded completely different from how Father said it. I know he used to love me. Maybe he still did, but he didn't know how to show it. Maybe he was scared to show love for anything else for fear that somehow I would be taken away from him, too.

But it had been many years since I had heard anyone speak to me with such tenderness. Except for Jesus. Once or twice, his voice had sounded almost like mother's.

I shook my head to put him out of my mind for the moment. "Where have you been, Mother? Have they treated you well?"

Her smile faded, and the light in her eyes darkened. "We will speak of that later. Right now," deliberately putting her smile back into place, "we will eat together. I have a small meal prepared for the slaves in my master's house. There is enough for you, too. He will not be there today, so we can talk. Unless your duties require you to be somewhere else?"

I saw the pleading in her eyes. She would not want to disturb a working man, but she also didn't want to let me go now that we had finally found each other. I felt the same way.

"I have not made any plans. I can preach just as well among your master's slaves as anywhere else. In fact, my Master instructed us to make no plans but to go wherever we're led to. It's very inefficient but allows for flexibility in cases such as these." I gave Mother a grin that she answered with her own.

"Then follow me, Son. We can talk later about the past. Tell me about your life now."

I told her of how I was called by Jesus and chosen to be one of his elite twelve.

Her eyes clouded when she heard about Father's continued debt. "Praise Adonai that the Romans didn't take you, too. Most slaves are male, because they get more work out of them and are stronger."

"Mother, who is your master?"

She smiled a sad smile. "I am a *servus publicus*, a public slave of the Roman Empire. I have no one owner, but I was bought by Brutus. He is responsible for my care and oversees my duties. He is a Roman official, but not in the military. He is not bad, as masters go. He treats us very well, rarely whipping or striking any of us. He has very little manual labor needing to be done, so I am blessed by Adonai that I am allowed to work as a seamstress for his many costumes of state as well as for his daughter. His wife had just died when he bought me at the slave market."

"The slave market! How barbaric!" Memories crowded into my mind of the Roman children hurling out insults to us Jewish boys, claiming we were all only fit to stand naked on the circular dais for showing off merchandise by the slave traders.

I tried to avoid the mental picture of my beautiful mother naked with the soldiers pointing out all her assets. My fists tightened. I wished I had been big enough and strong enough to give those Roman soldiers what for.

"It was humiliating, Son, yes. But Adonai protected me and blessed me with this position. I am almost happy now, if it weren't for the loneliness for you and not being allowed to celebrate Jewish holidays and customs. But enough about me. What are your duties to this Jesus of Nazareth?"

"I am the treasurer." My chest puffed out as I bragged about my position to my long-lost Mother. "I keep the funds safe, and I am responsible for buying our necessities at the lowest price possible. I'm a shrewd negotiator, if I do say so myself."

Mother smiled fondly, her parental pride filling my soul's holes that my father had left empty for more than a decade.

We had reached the house of the Roman magistrate. I followed Mother through the back entrance to the slave's quarters, where she poured water from the well into each cup and introduced me to each fellow slave.

I ate with them, laughing and joking around the rough, unsanded table, regaling them with many tales of the miracles Jesus had performed and some of the unusual messages he had taught.

When the others had to get back to their duties, I asked Mother if I might stay there for the night somewhere. She was ecstatic to welcome me. There was a small chamber near hers that was unused at the moment. She showed me where it was and then kissed me goodbye as she went back to work.

I left in the afternoon to do some more preaching. And donation seeking. When I mentioned that my mother had been taken from me as a boy and my father was in debt, I got even more sympathy tokens than usual. I wished I had thought to use my sob story before.

When I was dusty and tired and hungry again, and the sun was sending its setting rays during the warm, dry season right into my eyes, I headed back to my room for the night.

Mother met me at the door and offered to get me a loaf of bread. I accepted.

As I ate, I asked her to tell me about her life as a slave.

She explained, "When the soldiers were told of our family's debt, they were going to take your father as a slave. But Brutus knew who he was and knew that your father was not in great health and that they would not get much work out of him. He also knew that you and I would have almost no chance to survive without him. So he asked around in town for information about you and me. He thought you would be too weak for some of the manual labor you would most likely have to do. And he wanted to give you a chance to grow up with a more normal childhood, especially as a Jew. He is sympathetic to our people's religion."

I merely grunted. So what if he had seemed to have good intentions. He still made me grow up without a mother, a comforter, an encourager.

Mother continued. "So when several of the women in the marketplace told them that I was handy with a needle, he decided to make me the official seamstress for the municipal council and especially for all of his political costumes. I had it easy, Judas. I'm so thankful to Adonai that my job was not arduous nor immoral. I have never had to fear my master's hand. Brutus is a kind master, though he is not allowed to give us permission to attend Jewish feasts and Sabbath celebrations. But I could have had it much worse, Son. Adonai be praised."

A suspicion arose in my mind. "Just how kind is this Master Brutus, Mother? Does he have any ulterior motives with you?"

Because she flushed and looked down for a moment, I knew she understood my insinuation. "I believe he does look at me more fondly than any of the other women slaves here. But he has never acted on it. In fact, he is willing to let me go."

"What do you mean?"

She remained silent for a few moments, holding my gaze. I couldn't explain the look in her eyes as she continued, "I've been working for my *manumission.*"

"Your freedom? How? When?"

"The municipal council will allow slaves to be set free if their overseers have asked for it, and if they can prove our hardworking attitudes. Brutus has requested my freedom. I'm now in the process of proving my ability to be an upstanding citizen."

"How long will that take?"

"Who knows? It could take only weeks; it could take more than a year. However long the council needs."

"What will you do if you are released, Mother? Does Brutus think you will stay with him voluntarily? Or are you thinking of actually going back to Father?"

Her eyes clouded. Then she let out a long sigh. "I do not know for sure, my Son. But I am still married to him. In Adonai's sight, we are one."

I thought about that for a few moments. Faithfulness was commendable. But the practicality of remaining faithful to someone who was less than worthy made me wonder if Mother's faithfulness was a bit naive.

"Well, anyway, I have an even better idea. My master is going to be the Messiah, and when he overthrows Rome in Israel, I'll have a high position as his treasurer. Then I'll finally have the money to buy that piece of land I've been looking at. When I buy it, you and I will live there together, and I'll take better care of you than Father ever did."

"Oh, my son, don't resent him. Bitterness of soul is a disease that will hurt you far worse than it will ever hurt your father."

I felt a prick in my heart, but I pushed it away. "Mother, I have to leave soon. But let me know if you do earn your freedom. I'll come get you or meet you somewhere."

"My son, I will pray for your safety and for your new mission. I pray that Jesus of Nazareth will be the answer to all of your hopes."

All I could hope for at that time was my new land. It would solve all my problems. And Jesus would be the means to get it for me.

CHAPTER 7 THE FEEDING

After we all came back together, Jesus taught us privately. Then we headed to a small town called Bethsaida. The crowds found us there. Jesus led them up to the top of the mountain so he could teach and heal the sick.

Simon the Zealot and I dawdled behind the other disciples to resume our ongoing discussion.

"I can't wait until Jesus leads our revolt against Rome," murmured Simon, passion vibrating his low-pitched voice.

"I know," I agreed, keeping my voice low, too. We didn't want to be overheard by anyone loyal to Rome. I knew a few people had followed Jesus out of curiosity but left out of fear that he would bring retribution from the Romans. I kept following Jesus, hoping for some mention of a strategy to overthrow those violent, heathen Romans.

"Those filthy, greedy Romans," Simon spat out. "I don't understand why Jesus doesn't call them out for their heathen idol worship, especially of Caesar."

We both glanced around to make sure no one was listening. These followers were mostly like us who wanted a radical change in Israel's status as a conquered territory, but you never know who could be listening. The Romans rewarded Jews who turned in dissenters.

I stepped even closer to him to lower my volume even more. "Yes, I know. I wonder what's going to happen to the governors and soldiers already here. Maybe we'll get to take some revenge. If I ever find out who those soldiers were that manhandled my poor mother, I don't know what I'll do. Show them what it feels like somehow."

Sadness and fury enveloped me as I remembered again the centurion who had invaded our house all those years ago. My crying mother's face still visited me in my nightmares every so often.

"Guess what, Simon? I've found my mother!"

"What? Where?"

"In Ptolemais, when we were sent out. She's thriving, healthy, and just about to earn her freedom." The fury faded, and the sadness reluctantly gave way to hope. And pride in my strong mother for doing more than just surviving.

"That's great, Judas. At least one of us can move on."

I glanced at his face. His eyes held envy, not happiness for me. "What did the Romans do to you, anyway?"

Simon just shook his head. He still refused to tell me. Either he couldn't talk about it, or he thought I couldn't handle it. Or maybe he was in the wrong and thought I would sympathize with the Romans. What an idiot. Didn't he know how much I hated them, too?

Jesus looked out over the crowds and locked eyes with me. He beckoned us to come help with the rest of the disciples.

Simon immediately began talking about the weather. I shot him a glance that said, "Good going, Smarty. Couldn't you have picked a more subtle subject?"

Jesus wouldn't have been happy hearing about our thirst for vengeance. But he obviously had lived a sheltered, happy life for the most part with parents who loved him and cared for him. He had never suffered at the hands of the Romans like we had.

Jesus looked at us with that expression of knowing disappointment I knew so well. He often looked like that in his daily interactions with us disciples.

Did he know what we'd been talking about? Had he somehow heard? Or had one of the other do-good-er disciples snitched on us?

If Jesus knew we'd been plotting revenge, would he be upset enough to send us away?

Thankfully, he merely looked at us for a few moments with those disappointed but loving eyes. He turned to the rest of the disciples and announced that he wanted us to tell the crowds to sit in groups of hundreds and fifties.

That was an oddly specific request. I should have suspected he had some kind of plan in mind. But I was just glad he hadn't rebuked us for our vengeance or for trying to hide our conversation. I knew he hated deceit as much as anything else.

So as I was helping the elderly find the best seats on some of the rockiest places, I missed the signs of something big about to happen. He began healing all the sick that had been brought to him.

Then he taught. He taught for hours. We all tried to find little berries and snacks that had been brought. But as the afternoon was lengthening into evening, he paused and said something unusual.

He asked Philip if we had enough bread to feed them all. I snickered. We would have needed dozens of donkeys or camels to carry enough to feed all those people. Matthew and I had done the math and knew we had at least 5,000 men, but we didn't even bother counting the women taking care of the children who periodically got antsy and would run around behind the sitting men.

Philip was a little flustered. He wanted to make a good impression on our master, but he didn't have any way to feed them. He pointed to a boy with a burlap sack. "This boy has five loaves of bread and two small fishes. But what are they among so many?"

I had to agree with his defensive tone. There was nothing else he could have done. But surely Jesus knew that.

Jesus smiled his knowing smile, put his hand on the boy's head and whispered something in his ear. The boy beamed at him and held out the sack to Jesus.

Jesus took it and said, "Thank you, my boy. You shall be blessed for your faith and generosity."

Then he took each loaf of bread out of the sack, looked up to the sky, and prayed, "Father, thank you for your provision. May this bread be used to glorify your name."

Then he broke it into pieces and put into a basket. As he broke off each piece, I noticed that the loaf didn't seem to be getting much smaller. Eventually, the entire basket was full, and he still had half a loaf left.

I couldn't believe what I was seeing. He handed the first basket to Philip and told him to feed the people as much as they could eat.

Really? Even a whole basket wouldn't feed a hundred people as much as they could stuff themselves with. Maybe a few bites for everyone, if it was rationed out carefully.

He did that with each loaf and then with both fishes. We ended up with twelve baskets full. I know Philip had to scrounge around and ask some of the women for extra baskets.

Jesus gave each one of us twelve a basket to feed a group of hundred. When I passed mine around, I tried to stress that everybody needed to take only what would tide them over. But I still saw people in the middle of the rows taking more than I thought they should.

When the basket got through that hundred, it still wasn't even half empty. I took it to four groups of a hundred myself. When everyone had eaten their fill, there were some people calling out they had extra and someone else could have theirs.

So I went back through and collected all the leftovers. By this time, the smell of the bread and fish had made my stomach rumble. But Jesus wanted us to serve the people first. I had my doubts as to whether I would get any.

But when I got done collecting the leftovers, my basket was full. And when we all met down at the front, each of us had a full basket. We just looked at each other for several minutes. We were in awe.

But I was also starving. So I took the first bite. Shocked at how fresh it tasted, I mumbled, "Not bad, I guess."

I ate as much as I could. And I stuffed myself. I kept shoveling in bite after bite to see when the food would run out. It never did. I had to eventually put my hands on my stomach, groaning, and push away the still full basket.

We each had a full basket to take home to our families after we had eaten all we could.

I remembered the story in the writings of the prophets, when Elijah had made the last little bit of cake flour and oil last for months for a widow and her son.

Did this prove that Jesus was definitely a prophet? Was he the Prophet like Moses we all were looking for?

CHAPTER 8 THE STORM

Immediately, after this miracle of feeding more than 5,000, Jesus wanted us to get in the boats and go across the Sea of Galilee.

He said he would dismiss the crowds himself, but he wanted us to get away first.

Peter tried to argue, "But won't they ask you for more healing and teaching? Let us take care of dismissing them while you get away."

I thought his logic was sound. Jesus was much more likely to show compassion and give into helping them more than we thought he should. He needed some rest.

But he was determined to do it his way. He made us get in the boats. As the fishermen began rowing across the lake, I noticed some clouds forming on the horizon.

The Sea of Galilee is famous for its amazingly quick weather changes. One moment it's sunny and warm, and the next moment it's thundering and lightning. That's what happened that night.

We fought and fought against the wind all night. I think we must have gotten turned around a dozen times, for we never seemed any closer to land. Even the fishermen were looking grim and beginning to shake their heads, when, just before dawn, we saw something white on the lake coming toward us.

I thought at first it was another ship, though I couldn't figure out how it was moving so quickly against that strong wind, but then we realized it was a man. It was a man walking on top of the water!

"It must be a ghost!" cried James, as he dropped the oar and covered his eyes.

The man came close enough for us to hear his voice. He said, "Don't be afraid. It's me. Be courageous."

It was Jesus! Wait. Jesus could walk on top of water? Who is this guy?

And then Peter, ever the action-taker, climbs up on the edge of the boat and calls out, "If it's really you, Lord, bid me to come out to you on the water."

I couldn't decide if Peter was smart to ask for a sign of Jesus' identity or stupid for choosing a dangerous sign.

As he took a deep breath and put out his foot, I made up my mind. Yep, stupid. Peter was stupid.

But then he let go and stepped with his other foot. On the water. And he walked on the water toward Jesus! Our mouths were hanging open and eyes were bugging out. How in this physical world was it even possible? Would I have been able to step on top of the water if I had tried?

I felt an illogical desire to try. If Peter could do it, surely I could, too. Couldn't I?

I stood up to watch Peter's progress and made my way to the side where he'd stepped off. He was doing it. He was looking straight ahead at Jesus and walking on water. I made my way to the edge of the boat. I grabbed tightly to the rigging and tried to decide if I would follow Peter's stupid courage.

Then something happened. I saw his head turn, and he looked around at the high waves and the heavy rain. A lightning bolt lit up the scene. I will never forget the look of peace on Jesus' face and the absolute terror on Peter's.

Then he began to sink. He stopped walking and fell into the water! We all gasped. Now what?

Just before his head went under, Peter called out, "Save me, Lord!"

Immediately Jesus reached out his hand and was able to reach Peter and pull him up. He pulled Peter to his side and together they walked the rest of the way to the boat, though we were still rolling and pitching with the huge waves.

Jesus said to Peter, "You of little faith, why did you doubt?"

While Peter tried to stammer out a response, I wondered if Peter's faith was the thing that had helped him walk on the water in the first place. Maybe he had begun to sink because his faith had been shaken by thinking of the dangers of the storm.

If that was the case, I wouldn't have been able to walk on the water anyway. There's no way I could ever believe I was capable of miracles. No way!

But I envied Peter's faith. He had been the only one of us twelve to even try. I had to hand it to Peter. He sure was bold. But faith can seem an awful lot like stupidity. And I did not want to be thought stupid.

After all, what did walking on the water accomplish? How did it get any of us any closer to defeating Rome? How did it turn the tide of political popularity? It didn't. It didn't do anything.

What a waste of a miracle.

But as soon as Peter and Jesus climbed into the boat with us, the waves stilled and the wind stopped. The sun immediately shone through the clouds near the horizon. The storm was over.

Several disciples looked at each other and asked, "Who is this man that even the wind and waves obey him?" I wasn't convinced Jesus had had anything to do with the storm. It started suddenly, why couldn't it end suddenly?

James and John, Peter, and several others bowed down to Jesus and began worshiping him like he was a god! I was shocked at their blasphemy. It seemed that Jesus was definitely a prophet of God. But God himself? That's blasphemous!

I noticed that Thomas and Simon the Zealot also remained standing on the edge. We were the only ones who refused to be pulled into a blaspheming cult.

Would it be a good idea to get out now? I'm sure if the Pharisees ever discovered any of Jesus' disciples belief that he was a god, they would hang us all.

I would have to be extra wary now. On alert at all times. I would not be drawn into something that didn't stamp out the Romans from Israel as its primary goal.

We were then immediately at the shore somehow. Jesus said, "Let's all rest now in the boat, for the crowds will soon find us. Try to get a few hours' sleep, my friends."

Of course, there wasn't enough room on the boat for all of us to lay out comfortably. I got the worst part, the skinny end of the prow. I had to dangle my legs over the edge just so I had enough room to lay my head down on the hard wood.

Our few hours' sleep was restless, to say the least, but Jesus was right. It was all we got. Once the crowds realized that Jesus wasn't coming back to that side of the Sea, they all got in boats and followed us towards Capernaum.

When they found us, they began shouting, "Rabbi, when did you get here? We've been waiting for you!"

Jesus held up his hands and waited for them to quiet. He began answering as he led them to the synagogue in Capernaum. In an even voice he answered, "Truly, truly, I say that you're looking for me not because you realized what my signs and wonders meant. But you're only following me to get more food for your bellies."

Some began to murmur to themselves in disagreement, but Jesus ignored them and continued, "Don't work for temporary food that spoils quickly. Work instead for spiritual food that lasts for eternity. This is the kind of food I, the Son of Man, will give to you. For it's on me that the Father has placed his seal of approval."

This seemed awfully presumptuous to me. I think I saw a few looks by others who seemed to agree with me.

But a few of his most avid followers asked, "Well, how do we know what God requires of us then?"

Jesus smiled that sad smile again. He was disappointed that they didn't understand yet. But he seemed to have expected it. He answered,

"The work of God is simply to believe on Him who has been sent by Him."

By this time, we had reached the synagogue.

"You?" someone in the back called, in a tone of disbelief. "What sign are you giving us to prove that you've been sent by God Himself? Our fathers in the wilderness were given bread from heaven, the manna was given directly by God. Why should we believe that the loaves and fishes came from God when they came through you?"

Jesus sighed and responded, "Truly, truly, I say to you..." He sure loved to use that phrase. That had become his catch-phrase. I wondered why he chose that one. Maybe it's because he was trying get us to really search for the truth.

"Truly, truly, I say to you, that it wasn't Moses who gave you the bread from heaven. It was my Father who gave the true bread from heaven. And it's the true bread that gives life to the world."

Several of the most vocal followers called out, "Give us this kind of bread always then!"

I know I wasn't the only one who was shocked when Jesus answered, "I am the bread of life."

And he used the phrase, "I am!" That's Adonai's name! That's blasphemy again!

But Jesus kept right on adding insult to injury. "Whoever comes to me won't ever go hungry, and those who believe in me won't ever be thirsty. But you have seen me and my works, and you still refuse to believe. All those the Father gives to me I will keep. I haven't come down from heaven to do my own will, but I am here to do my Father's will only, because He's the One who sent me. I won't lose any of those He has given to me because it's His will for me to keep them until I raise them up in the last days. Everyone who believes in the Son will have eternal life, and I will raise them up on the last day."

What was he trying to do, alienate everyone who had been following him? Come on, Jesus, I thought, have a little tact, a little shrewdness. You can't lead a nation if no one wants you to lead!

The crowd of true Jews was offended at this saying, and rightfully so. They turned to each other and complained, "Isn't this Jesus the son of Joseph the carpenter? We know his mother and father, so how can he say that he came down from heaven? He must be either crazy or a liar!"

Then Jesus added the final straw. "Stop grumbling among yourselves. No one can come to me unless the Father draws them to me, and I will raise all of them He sends me at the last day. It is written in the Prophets, 'They will all be taught by God.' No one has seen the Father, except for me whom He has sent. If anyone believes in me, they have eternal life, because I am the bread of life. You fathers did eat manna in the wilderness, but they still died. But here with you now is bread from heaven that will keep anyone from dying who eats it. Whoever eats of this bread will live forever. This bread is my flesh, and I will give it up for the world to have life."

Some of the crowd wanted to believe in him, that he came directly from the Father in heaven. But others argued loudly with them, "How can he give us his flesh to eat? That's cannibalism! How disgusting! That's not of God!"

If Jesus had just remained quiet, some of the discontented might have been silenced by the most ardent believers. They kept trying to reason that Jesus meant eating his flesh figuratively, metaphorically. But he couldn't keep his mouth shut and kept speaking.

"Truly, truly, I say to you, you must eat of my flesh and drink of my blood to inherit eternal life. If you don't, you will have no life. For my flesh is real food and my blood real drink, whoever eats my flesh and drinks my blood abides in me, and I live in them, too. This is the bread from heaven."

Even his most vocal proponents and us apostles were shocked and said, "This is a really hard teaching! Can anyone accept it?"

Jesus heard us and looked right at each of us twelve. "Does this offend you?" Most of us just looked down, but Peter boldly shook his head. What a liar and a brown-noser.

"What if you were to see the Son of Man ascend back into heaven? The flesh doesn't count for anything, but the Holy Spirit gives life. These words I've spoken to you have been full of Spirit and of life. But you won't accept them, because you're not of the Spirit. There are some of you who do not believe."

He looked right at me again with that sad look in his eyes. I know I wasn't the only one who didn't believe him. Why did he single me out? Was he trying to shame me into submission? I rebelled against manipulation. I'd been controlled all my life. I was through being manipulated.

Many of his followers left in disgust and never came back. Even one of his most avid followers looked sorrowfully at Jesus in rebuke, then turned and shuffled away.

Jesus turned back to us twelve and asked softly, "Are you wishing to leave me, too?"

I was tempted. Boy, did I want to just give up and go home. Following Jesus wasn't comfortable. We never knew where we going to sleep. We never knew when we would get our next meal. And Jesus' teaching often left me uncomfortable. But this teaching was the worst.

I didn't know if it was worth it to follow him anymore. He was obviously losing followers and political clout. He was making too many enemies. He hadn't been shaking enough influential hands and kissing enough babies.

How would we ever gain support from the people now?

But then again, I had already given him months out of my life. I had ascended to a place of honor as one of his chosen few. Maybe I could stick it out a little longer and see if maybe he bounced back. And if I stuck it out longer than the others, then surely I would be rewarded with higher honors and titles and places of power.

I hoped that some of the twelve would leave then. It would give me an advantage. What if the loyal three—Peter, James, and John—turned on him and weren't loyal anymore?

But Peter, Mr. Bigmouth, ruined my hopes by stepping forward. He began with addressing him as, "Lord," using the Greek version of the sacred name of Yahweh, the name we don't even speak with our lips! "Lord, who else would we go to? You are the one who has the words of eternal life."

Peter spread out his arms and presumed to include all the rest of us in his sweeping statement, "We already believed and knew that you are the Holy One of God!"

Jesus smiled at him, pleased with this declaration. He looked around and said, "Haven't I chosen you Twelve?"

But he knew not all of us would go so far. His eyes landed on me once again, and his smile faded. "But one of you is a false accuser, a liar."

There he was, singling me out again! Well, I'd show him! I would stay longer than anyone else and prove my worthiness. I would prove that my cunning was way more beneficial to a political leader than Peter's over-the-top blustering or John's wimpy, yes-man, hero worshiping.

Then he would reward me! And I would deserve it!

CHAPTER 9 THE MEETING

While I was out on a shopping trip for food and supplies in Capernaum, I made a short detour to the synagogue.

I had to negotiate a bit but finally got a short meeting with one of the Pharisees. At first, he looked with disgust at a dirty, bedraggled commoner.

"My name is Judas Iscariot. I am one of the Twelve chosen disciples of Jesus of Nazareth."

Then his eyes widened in recognition of Jesus' name and his nostrils flared., in contempt. "Jesus of Nazareth is a rabble-rouser, stirring up the people to believe blasphemous things. If you're one of his followers, why are you here?"

"I may have been misled by my expectations of him. I believed at first that he might be the Messiah, come to take back Israel from Rome. He was gaining popularity with the common people. But his teaching is one of 'turning the other cheek,' of loving your enemy and paying your taxes. I'm not so sure he's willing to try to take on the Roman Empire. Even if he wanted to, he doesn't have an army or even anyone who knows how to use a sword, except maybe one."

The Pharisee raised an eyebrow. "If these are your thoughts, why follow him still?"

What a crafty, wily, old geezer. "A very cunning question, sir. I will still follow him until I find something better. At least right now, he lets me take care of the money. I make sure we have enough food to eat. I wasn't guaranteed that much at home."

"I see." He stroked his beard for a few moments and then asked, "So what is it that you want with me?"

"Sir, I wanted to ask if there was anything I could do for you. I have noticed that you scribes and Pharisees have been trying to trap Jesus with his own words, trying to trip him up with regards to the law or theology."

"And what is that to you?"

"Well, I've also noticed that you haven't gotten anywhere with it. All questions are either deflected with an answering question, answered with a hard-to-understand parable, or completely ignored as he changes the subject."

"Yes, yes, yes. I know this already. What is your point?"

I cleared my throat to give me time to think about my next move. "My point is that I think I may have some knowledge about Jesus that would be valuable to you. I know his whereabouts all the time. I know his habits of both solitary prayer and charismatic ministry. I know which subjects he would likely avoid talking about. I think I can help you talk him into a corner, provide you with enough evidence to arrest him."

"Do you think so? Why should I trust a man willing to turn on his own master? What keeps you from turning on me?"

I swallowed the bile that rose in throat. I outwardly curbed my annoyance that he would dare accuse me of treachery even before discussing a deal. What a weasel.

"I believe, shrewd sir, that you understand that you have an opportunity with me you won't find anywhere else. I don't know how to swear my allegiance to the deal when we haven't discussed a price. Perhaps if I were satisfied with a substantial enough sum, I would not afford to back out."

"Ah, here we go. I can see you are a shrewd negotiator. But you are getting ahead of yourself. I have never said that I am willing to pay for your services. I personally believe that we Pharisees, working together with the scribes and chief priests, will be able to take down Jesus of Nazareth quite easily without you. I fear an inside man would be too risky. If something went wrong, if you made one small comment, all would be lost. He would go into hiding, and though we have a far reach, we cannot be in every place."

He stroked his beard again and then stood. "No, I'm afraid this meeting is at an end. There is nothing you can do for us that we can't do for ourselves. And definitely not something we need to outsource. We will keep our money, thank you. Let me have you escorted out."

I spun on my heels and stomped out, livid at my dismissal. I was offering the easy way out. Surely, that should have been worth something to him.

Apparently these Pharisees were dumber than I had taken them for.

CHAPTER 10 THE TRANSFIGURATION

About a week or so after the miracle of the loaves and fishes and the subsequent paring down of followers, Jesus took us up to a high mountain.

Or, I should say, he left nine of us at the bottom and took his favorite three up to a high mountain. Peter, James, and John always got the best stuff and the most time with Jesus. I wonder why they were so special.

Anyway, while they were up there, a crowd gathered around us and began clamoring for the miracle-worker. One man in particular needed Jesus to heal his son, a lankly teenager.

The father explained, "My son has a spirit that prevents the boy from talking. He's a mute. And the spirit often seizes control of his body and throws him down on the ground, foaming at the mouth and grinding his teeth. We can't do anything with him when he's like that. I live in constant fear that the evil spirit will harm my boy or even kill him! Please help us!"

I stepped forward, determined to be useful to Jesus and win his favor. "Jesus is up on the mountain right now and has forbidden anyone to come up after him. But we all have cast out demons before. Let us try."

"Oh, could you? Thank you so much, sir! We're at our wits end trying just to keep him alive. Please heal him!"

I waved the other disciples over to the boy, and we all laid our hands on his head. The boy was quiet. He didn't try to impede us, but he didn't do anything to help, either.

After a few moments, I began praying aloud, "Adonai Almighty, you have given us the power to cast out demons before. Do so now for this boy."

The crowd pressed in to see if it had worked. Nothing happened.

I asked the boy to speak. He opened his mouth but no sound came. His father shifted his weight from foot to foot, clearing his throat.

I nodded at Matthew, and he did the same thing, praying aloud and then commanding the boy to speak. Nothing happened.

Simon the zealot and Thomas both took turns. Our prayers got louder and more dramatic. But nothing worked.

Some of the crowd began to murmur against us. We began to hear shouts of "Try again" and "Go get Jesus" and "Is something supposed to happen?" Some of the hecklers began to laugh at the more witty pieces of "advice."

I was getting angry. We had done everything we had done before when Jesus had sent us out. We had been commissioned by Jesus to be his helpers. Why wouldn't God answer our demands for healing?

A niggling doubt kept bothering me. What if this proved that Jesus wasn't really sent of God? But then how had he cast out demons? And how had we cast out demons, then?

The father's shoulders sagged, and his head dropped to his chest, the picture of hopelessness.

I looked at the other disciples, and they all shrugged their shoulders. None of us knew what else to do.

Finally I heard a disturbance at the edge of the crowd closest to the path from the mountain. I couldn't see from where I was, in the middle of the crowd wanting to see a miracle, but I thought I heard the name Jesus.

Finally! Jesus and the three had returned. The father left us and ran to Jesus himself. I could just barely hear him exclaim, "Rabbi, I had brought my demon-possessed, mute, deaf son to you for healing."

Oh, he had failed to mention to us that the boy was deaf, too. No wonder he hadn't helped or responded in any way. That would have been helpful to know.

"The spirit throws him on the ground, foaming at the mouth. Can you heal him? Your disciples sure couldn't, though I asked them to spare you the trouble."

I looked at Thomas, and we both rolled our eyes. We knew that's not exactly how it happened.

The crowd had now allowed Jesus to make his way to the man's son. He glanced at us remaining nine disciples and asked, "O faithless generation, how long must I put up with you? Bring him here."

Thomas and Simon the Zealot helped the boy stand up and continued to support him. Maybe that was my mistake. I had just met him where he sat on the ground. Maybe a person had to stand if he could.

As soon as the boy looked Jesus in the face, the spirit inside threw him to the ground, and he began convulsing, rolling about and foaming at the mouth. It was a terrible sight to behold.

Jesus put his hand on the father's shoulder and compassionately asked, "How long has he been this way?"

"Since he was a small child, years and years ago. It has often thrown him into fires and water, trying to kill him. But if you can do anything for him, please have mercy on us and help him!"

"If I can? Yes, I can. All things are possible to the one who believes."

The father looked into Jesus' eyes, and his eyes lit up with hope. He clasped his hands together in pleading, "I believe, Teacher! Help my unbelief!"

Jesus patted his back and smiled reassuringly. He turned to the child and said, "You mute and deaf spirit, I command you to come out of him. And never enter into him again."

The spirit cried out in the boy's voice, convulsing him even more violently, and then suddenly stopped. The boy was so completely still and looked so much like a corpse that the nearest bystanders began to murmur, "He's dead!" A couple looked at Jesus like he had been the cause of death.

The scene had been so horrible that my mind had gone into survival mode, just being an unemotional observer. But once the spirit was cast out, I had time to think.

Jesus hadn't done anything extra special. He hadn't even laid hands on the boy, like he had taught us to do. He didn't touch his tongue or his ears like he had done to a few other mutes.

In fact, the only thing he had done was speak directly to the spirit. But the other disciples and I had spoken directly to God like Jesus had taught us. Wouldn't the spirit be more likely to respond to God than us? Or Jesus?

Then Jesus reached down, took the boy's hand, and lifted him up. The boy stood up with color in his cheeks again.

The father hugged his son, and the son calmly said, "Father! I'm okay now." The crowd began to cheer. Many began singing psalms of praise to God, extolling His majesty and thanking Him for using Jesus to heal this boy.

Jesus then made his way back to the town to find a house to sleep in that night. One in the crowd pushed his way up to me and said, "Tell your master that I would be honored for him to stay in my house tonight. And all of you disciples can stay in my stables."

I pushed past Peter and James on his left and relayed the man's message. Jesus graciously accepted and asked the man to lead the way.

When we got there and Jesus had sent away the crowd, the man invited us to wait in the house until after a meal. While he was in the next room explaining the situation to his poor wife, I turned to Jesus and asked, a little defensively, "Why couldn't I cast out that demon? Why couldn't any of us? We all tried. We all did just like you taught us."

Jesus looked at me for several moments. I began to squirm under the scrutiny. He finally answered, "This kind of demon can't be driven out by anything but prayer and fasting."

"How will we know to be fasting ahead of time for this kind of healing?" I thought it was unfair to rebuke us for not being able to do something that requires fasting, but we didn't have time to fast.

"Did you believe that you could cast the demon out?"

Jesus answered a question with another question, a teaching strategy he used often, but it drove me crazy. Couldn't he just answer an honest question with a straight answer?

"Yes," I said, making excuses. "We've done it before. We should have been able to do it this time. I didn't know there were different kinds of demons and varying methods."

Then Thomas spoke up and asked, "If we believed we could, why couldn't we?"

Jesus answered, "Because your little faith was in the wrong object. You were trusting in yourselves. In a method. In past experience. But a humble healer always has faith in the only constant—God our Healer, Adonai Raphta. For truly, truly, I say to you that if you only have faith as small as a grain of mustard seed in the Almighty God, you could say to that mountain, 'Move from here to there,' and it would move. Then nothing would be impossible for you."

For several long moments, I was busy digesting this extravagant promise and trying to decide if this was more of his hyperbole he loved so much or if he was literally saying we had the power to move mountains.

Before I could come to any conclusions, Peter again opened his big mouth and said, "Yes, nothing is impossible with you, Master. Our experience on the Mount taught us that." He exchanged knowing looks with James and John. James gave him a warning look.

Simon the zealot leaned forward and asked, "What happened up there?"

Peter smirked and put his finger his lips. "Sorry, I can't tell you. The Master has forbidden us to tell anyone what happened. That includes you nine, too, I guess."

Leave it to Peter to lord it over us that he got to do something with Jesus that we didn't and then not even satisfy our curiosity about it. What an arrogant prick.

Why does Peter get to have all the fun? Why do James and John get to always sit the closest to Jesus and talk with him the most? Why do they get to have the most input and influence with our Master? He chose all of us twelve specially.

I've always loathed teacher's pets.

CHAPTER 11 THE GREATEST

The rainy season began. In late fall, we now had to walk through the rain and mud everywhere. As we were sloshing to the next town, Jesus talked about many things.

He mentioned divorce again. This time he used the words: "What therefore God has joined together, let not man separate."

I remembered what Mother had said about possibly returning to Father. It seemed my Master would agree with her that they were still one flesh. Poor Brutus. He was freeing her only to lose her forever to another man, the man who had gotten her into that mess in the first place.

Jesus then went on to prophesy again about him being spit on and flogged and killed and then raised on the third day. We still had no idea what he was talking about.

But after he finished predicting his death, or whatever lesson he was trying to teach us, James and John pushed past the rest of us and walked alongside Jesus. I was near enough to hear the entire conversation.

James began, "Master, we want you to do something for us."

That didn't sound like an auspicious beginning to me. If anyone were to start a conversation with that line, I would automatically want to say no.

But Jesus didn't flinch. He merely asked, "What do you want me to do for you?"

John spoke up and wheedled, "Please give one of us your right hand seat and the other your left hand seat in your kingdom."

How dare they? Already asking for positions of authority and power! What if other disciples were more deserving, like me? How dare they get in first and call "dibs" on these places of honor!

Jesus didn't get upset, he just said, "You don't know what you're asking. Can you drink the cup I drink and be baptized with the same baptism as me?"

James and John both assured him, "Of course we're able! Absolutely!"

Jesus shook his head and replied, "Yes, you will drink the same cup and be baptized with the same baptism. But it's not my place to give the places of honor. That's for the Father to decide."

Peter and Thomas had heard and began murmuring to the other disciples. Eventually all ten of us were complaining, "They shouldn't be asking that yet! How ambitious! Brown-nosers!"

Jesus stopped walking and waited until he had our full attention. Then he used this conversation as a teaching tool.

"You know how the Gentiles lord their authority over those underneath them? My kingdom will be different. If you want to be the greatest in it, you will need to be a servant. The servant of all will be the greatest of all. For even I, the Son of Man, came not to be served but to serve and to give his life as a ransom for many."

Peter asked, "So who will be the greatest in your kingdom, then?"

You'd think by this time he would have learned to keep his mouth shut a little better. But no. He had to open his mouth and insert his foot again.

Jesus gave him a long, sad look, so long that Peter began shifting his weight and looking at anything else besides those piercing brown eyes.

Jesus finally sighed and answered, "You want to know who's going to be greatest, Peter? I'll show you."

He walked down the road, and we all followed, curious.

When he came upon some children playing in the streets, he called them over and knelt down to talk to them. He smiled and asked a little girl, "Would you talk to my friends for just a minute? It won't take long, and I promise you'll be safe."

She took her hand away from her mouth and smiled a dirty, toothless smile. Jesus stood up, offered his hand to her, and then led her right into the middle of us twelve. We crowded around to make sure we heard this. Maybe Jesus was going to tell us who he had chosen to be his cabinet members.

"Truly, truly, I say to you, if you don't turn around and become like these little children, you won't see the kingdom of heaven."

Jesus put his hand on her dark curls and smiled again, then told her she could go. She smiled back and then skipped back to her friends.

We looked at each other. What had he meant? How did we need to be like little children to see his kingdom? What quality about little children was Jesus even talking about?

I sure didn't want to be a snot-nosed kid again. And I didn't want to be stepped on and cast away and made to work as hard as a slave, like most children.

Bartholomew asked, "Is it because they're so honest? Or because of their humility?"

Jesus smiled, pleased with him, and answered, "Yes, both. You must come with the simple faith of a child. Leave your skepticism and self-deception behind. Be like a child again."

He looked around at each of us, and when he came to me, he held my eyes a little longer than the rest, I thought. Did he think I needed this lesson more than the brash Peter? Or the skeptical Thomas? Was that fair?

CHAPTER 12 THE SINNERS

Despite Jesus' controversy, or maybe because of it, we had even greater crowds pressing around us day after day. One day, as we were passing through Jericho, so many people lined the city streets that we could barely move.

Many children pushed their way to the front to be able to see a glimpse of the famous Jesus of Nazareth. But there was another man who was so short that he couldn't see over the shoulders of normal adults.

I didn't notice anything out of the ordinary until Jesus stopped altogether and looked up into a fig-mulberry tree nearby. At first, we disciples were worried about some kind of assassination attempt. Simon the zealot and I were scanning the area for a way of escape, when Jesus shouted up toward the bough of the tree, "Zaccheus, hurry and come down from there. I need to stay at your house today."

That was a little unusual, but nothing shocking. We often stayed in strangers' homes. They usually asked us, though, instead of Jesus inviting us into their homes.

But Zaccheus seemed genuinely happy about the invitation. He almost skipped down the road to his house, chattering with Jesus the whole way. I didn't bother trying to follow his rambling.

It wasn't until we were seated at his table for the evening meal that we heard grumblings of Jesus' partiality.

After the meal was over, Thomas went outside to help the servants bring in enough water for our trip through this extremely hot part of the country. When he came back in, he whispered to Simon and me, "The crowds outside are complaining. They said Jesus has entered the house of a sinner."

"Why, what's he done?" I whispered back.

Thomas glanced at Matthew, who fortunately was too far away to hear. He covered his mouth with his hand and whispered, "He's a tax collector." Then he made a big show of wiping his hand on his napkin and clearing his throat.

I thought about tax collectors. In general, they were greedy thieves and traitors who squeezed every shekel out of their own people. They lined their own pockets before handing the remainder over to the Romans for them to finance wars and keep us under their thumbs.

It galled me that Jesus would be associated with traitors. Matthew was bad enough. But another one? Just because Levi had been turned into Matthew and seemed to be a new man doesn't mean that all tax collectors could reform. He was most likely an exception.

Wouldn't the people get the idea that Jesus was more for Rome than for overthrowing it? Maybe that was Jesus' scheme, to act like he was for Rome and gain their trust before he exposed and destroyed them all.

This theory satisfied me, at least until Zaccheus stood up and made a speech. "Lord, look upon me and see my good intentions. I will give half of my goods to the poor. And I know I have defrauded many people. Where I have kept records, I will restore it four times what I cheated them."

I was shocked! This was the most unusual event of the entire day. Here Zaccheus was favored by Jesus and he turns around and offers to pay retribution?

How would Jesus finance his new regime if all of his closest advisers gave away all their money? I surely didn't have any to offer. And I knew the fisherman didn't either.

What little I did have I needed to save. Who knew when we would be asked to feed 5,000 men again without a boy's lunch to work a miracle with.

I had to admit to myself that I admired Zaccheus for sacrificing so much to follow Jesus. I never had enough money to give. I was always the one required to accept charity. I knew how humiliating that was.

If I had as much as Zaccheus, though, I don't know that I could give it up so easily. I would want to save it for a rainy day. Wouldn't that be the prudent thing to do?

Of course, it was a good thing to help the poor. But paying back what you'd cheated people out of already? That seemed a little excessive. Surely just apologizing would be enough. And then avoiding falling back into that sin. Wouldn't that be enough to show he's been accepted by Jesus?

Deep in my heart, I knew that Zaccheus was doing the right thing. But I disliked the implication that retribution was a prerequisite for following Jesus. I knew I had pilfered a few coins from my father to keep him from gambling all of it away.

Did this mean Jesus would expect me to pay my father back, too? I didn't know how I would pay for his debts and then mine on top of all that.

The familiar weight of financial burden settled on my back. I always carry stress in my back. Guilt too.

Now I knew why Jesus hadn't told me about the sacrifice part of following him. If I had known that, I don't think I would have taken that risk.

Well, it was too late at that point. I guess I would need to make some big donation or be a testimonial for reform to prove that I was an asset to Jesus. Just like any politician, he would want people to either love him or hate him, and it was our job to spread the word to those who would be most likely to accept it. That made sense from a networking point of view. Why didn't Jesus stick to my genius marketing plan?

I had reason to repeat this wail after Jesus talked to the Samaritan woman and all the Samaritans in her village. Then there was the Gentile woman from Tyre and Sidon who talked about even the Gentile dogs eating crumbs from the table of the Jews. And the Roman soldier who just asked Jesus to heal by word and believed that his servant would be healed by proxy.

Jesus, though mostly ministering to us Jews, still had more dealings with Gentiles than any other Jew was comfortable with. It would eventually get him in trouble with the Pharisees.

CHAPTER 13 THE DECLARATION

As we left that area and traveled to another city, we straggled out along the road like usual.

But Jesus stopped in the middle of nowhere and waited until all of us had gathered around, and he had our full attention. Then he asked, "Who do people say I am?"

That was an easy question. "Some say you're Elijah!"

"Some say you're John the Baptist!"

I answered, "Some say you're the Prophet we've been waiting for."

I agreed with those who guessed the Prophet, too, but I didn't include myself in this group, in case we were wrong.

Then Jesus asked, "But who do you say I am?"

Peter had to get his two cents in. He answered, "You are the Messiah, the Christ, the Son of the living God."

"That's going a little far, isn't it, Peter?" I scolded with an indulgent smile. Sometimes the only way to deal with Peter is to treat him like an errant child who hasn't learned to keep his mouth shut yet.

I heard Thomas and Simon murmur in agreement. But Jesus ignored us. He didn't even look my way or acknowledge my words in any way.

He looked only at Peter. "Very good, Peter. You haven't come up with that on your own. Neither has any person uncovered this truth. My Father in heaven has revealed it to you."

So Peter got something right? No wonder Jesus praised him. It didn't happen very often.

Unfortunately, that meant that I was wrong. I didn't like that. Not that I can't admit when I'm wrong. But that time I thought for sure I was right. The Prophet alluded to in the Old Testament might or might not be the Messiah.

We had grown up with predictions of the Messiah conquering Rome and freeing the Jews from the rule of the Gentiles. How could a Prophet of God also lead a revolution?

I guess we had several prophets in our history who were warriors, but mostly just the old judges before we had kings, like Gideon, Deborah and Barak, Jehud, and Samson. But except for Deborah the prophetess, the judges were not considered prophets.

None of the major and minor prophets were military men, like Isaiah, Jeremiah, Daniel, Ezekiel, Amos, Obadiah, Jonah, and all the rest. Only Nehemiah had really fought in any battle.

As I rehearsed this history lesson in my mind, I saw Peter's chest puff out.

But Jesus warned, "Don't tell anyone I'm the Messiah, though."

Why did he keep doing that? If we were going to start a revolution, we needed the common people to know who he was and that he was worthy of being followed. If he was going to be Israel's champion, he needed Israel to back him.

"The Messiah, the Son of the Living God." What did Peter mean by "the Son of the Living God"? God has always been living. I guess he wanted to stress that he was talking about the One true God, not any Greek mythology or Roman pantheon of gods, false gods.

But what did Jesus mean by agreeing with the title of Son? He liked to call himself the Son of Man. But the Son of God was a blasphemous title. It put him on equal footing with God, as one of his intimate family. Of course, he called God his Father all the time. But that was a metaphor, wasn't it?

CHAPTER 14 THE RESURRECTION & THE LIFE

I think Jesus had mentioned possibly being killed a time or two before. But I thought he was just speaking in hyperbole again.

However, this time he came right out and plainly said, "I'm going to go to Jerusalem and there I'm going to be killed. But don't worry, because I'll come to life again on the third day."

He couldn't really mean he was going to be put to death, because that would mean he was literally going to come back to life again, too. He had to have been speaking metaphorically.

Regardless, whatever his "death" meant, it wasn't good for me. It meant that all my hopes about a new regime, the overthrow of Rome, my new place of influence, and my new land and reputation would die with him.

One time when he again brought up his death, he told us that it would be the doing of the chief priest and scribes. They would have him killed. But he would rise again on the third day.

How in the world could he know this?

At this, Peter rebuked our Master, "Never, Lord! This won't ever happen to you! We won't let it!"

It looked like Peter wanted to be teacher's pet again. I knew he was fishing for more praise.

I chuckled when Jesus turned on Peter and rebuked him, "Get behind me, accuser. You're working for Satan. He's trying to use you to ensnare me and block my path. You don't have the concerns of God in mind. You're only thinking of mere human, earthly concerns."

I was glad Jesus had given Peter a talking to. He needed to be taken down a peg or two. But then Jesus went on to say what made my stomach knot.

"If you want to truly be my disciple, then you must deny yourself and take up your cross and follow me. If you want to save your life, you must lose it. If you lose your life for me, you will find life."

There he was speaking in riddles again. How could I gain life if I lost it? Was he talking about death? Would I have to die with him to gain the life I wanted? How could that be?

I didn't understand what he meant by this "life," I guess.

Jesus continued, "What good would it be for you to gain the whole world but forfeit your soul? What can anyone exchange for their soul?"

He went on to talk about himself as the Son of Man, and something about angels in the clouds, but I tuned him out. I was still stuck on giving up everything to follow him. Was he saying that there was no way to gain the power and wealth I wanted in this life? At least, not as his disciple.

Maybe that meant I should quit being his disciple. If he wasn't even promising a new kingdom anymore, if the "kingdom of God" he was always talking about wasn't the kingdom of Israel, then what was I still doing here?

My whole reason for following him was being stripped away. What else did that leave me? Self-denial and "death," even just a metaphorical death to my hopes and dreams, weren't a big enough inducement for me to stay.

I had just begun to wonder how I would leave, if I would need to talk to Jesus first or if I could find a time to sneak away without explaining myself to anyone, when a messenger came running up to us.

"Your dear friends Mary and Martha pleaded with me to tell you that their brother, your dear friend Lazarus, is deathly sick."

I knew how much Jesus loved that family. We often stayed at their house in Bethany when we came to Jerusalem.

I fully expected Jesus to immediately pack up and have us all travel as fast as possible to get there. But he took a breath and said calmly, "Lazarus will not end in death. This sickness has happened for the glory of God."

We stayed for two more days before he finally said, "Okay, now we can go back into Judea."

Peter miraculously kept his mouth shut this time. It was the other Simon, my friend the zealot, who said, "But Master, a few days ago, the Jews in Judea were trying to stone you! Are you sure it's safe to go back now?"

Jesus answered something about working while you have the light. What did that have to do with anything?

Then Jesus said, "Our friend Lazarus has fallen asleep, so I will go and wake him up."

I spoke up, "Lord, if he is sleeping, then that's good. He will soon get better." How could he know from so far away whether Lazarus was sleeping or not?

Maybe we shouldn't interrupt the healing a good night's rest would do. Especially if it might cost us being stoned.

Jesus looked at me. "Lazarus is dead. And for your sakes, I'm glad I didn't go. Now you'll see and truly believe. Come on, let's go see him."

Then good ole Thomas spoke up and said a bit sarcastically, "Well, if we die, we die. Let's go share his destiny."

When we finally arrived at Bethany two days later, we were told that Lazarus had already died and been buried four days ago. He must have died just after we got the message. Even if Jesus had left as soon as he got the message, we wouldn't have been in time.

I felt relieved. We were absolved from responsibility. Nothing we could have done would have made any difference. It had been Lazarus' time to die.

I don't know why Jesus could have sounded so certain. "Lazarus will not end in death."

For once it seemed Jesus had been wrong. Though I had gloated when Peter was proved wrong, Jesus being wrong struck me hard. I don't know why. I know he had already disappointed me in my dreams. But this was different. This seemed to be a direct contradiction to his very words.

I probably could have sneaked away at this point. Nobody was paying any attention to me. But I had to know what would happen. I needed to know how Jesus would react, and how the people would react to Jesus. My curiosity held me, though my stomach was queasy.

Before we got to their house, Martha came out to meet Jesus. But Mary decided to stay inside, whether to be polite to the mourners and guests or because she was mad at Jesus, I'll never know.

Martha seemed bitter, and she vocalized it. "Lord, if you had only gotten here in time, I know you could have healed our brother. I know he wouldn't have died. But even now, I believe that God will give you whatever you ask."

Why didn't she just come out and ask him to raise her brother from the dead? That's basically what it would take to do anything at this point, Lady.

Jesus wiped away a tear from her eyes, looked at her compassionately and told her, "Lazarus will rise again."

"Yes, Lord," answered Martha more meekly. "I know he will rise at the last day with everyone else in the final Resurrection."

Except for the Sadducees, who say there is no resurrection at all, no spiritual plane at all, everyone there probably agreed with Martha. I know I did. We had all been taught since before we could remember that the Law spoke of a bodily resurrection.

I couldn't see Jesus' face. I slowly made my way through the crowd behind Martha so I could see his expression. He glanced at me, like he knew what I was doing, smiled sadly, and then turned back to Martha.

I couldn't believe what he said next. And he said it like it was no big deal, like it was just another fact about himself.

"I am the resurrection and the life. Anyone..." and he glanced back at me before continuing, "anyone who believes in me will have life, even after death. Everyone who believes in me will never die." He placed his hands on her shoulders and looked deep into her eyes, digging into her soul. "Do you believe me, Martha?"

What would she say? What would I say if he asked me? I just didn't know. My mind was so staggered that I couldn't even think straight. I pulled myself out of the situation and became a mere observer again. It was safer that way.

Martha took a deep breath and replied, "Yes, Lord, I have believed—and still do believe—that you are the Messiah. You are the Son of God, the one who has come from God into the world."

Jesus touched her cheek and smiled, a radiance in his eyes at odds with the mourning around him. But it wasn't disrespectful at all.

In fact, as soon as Martha made this amazing declaration (how did she come to this conclusion, anyway?), she returned to the house and must have told Mary that Jesus wanted to see her, because it didn't take long for her come out to meet us.

Mary came almost at a run, fell at Jesus' feet, and began weeping. "Lord, if you had been here, my brother wouldn't have died."

They were the same words Martha had used, but Mary was the more emotional of the two. Before Jesus could answer, the mourners who had seen her leave, assumed she was going to mourn at Lazarus' tomb and followed her.

Now there was a large, loud crowd. I could tell that Jesus was trouble by Mary's sobbing. He looked like he was getting ready to unleash his tongue on the crowd of paid, insincere mourners, actors playing a part.

Instead, he asked, "Where is his tomb?"

And the neighbors said, "Follow us, we'll show you!"

Jesus turned and followed them, hugging Mary's shoulders. She was almost beside herself by this time. And Jesus wept with her.

I don't ever remember seeing Jesus weep before. The crowd around me kept whispering, "See how much Jesus loved him!"

I didn't think he was weeping for Lazarus as much as he was weeping for Mary.

Some of the skeptics murmured, "If he healed the blind man, couldn't he have kept this man from dying, if he had been here?" I didn't like the implication that Jesus really didn't have the power to heal but instead was a con man, maybe that the blind man's healing was just a hoax.

But hadn't I been thinking pretty much the same thing?

We reached the cave, and a large stone lay in front of it to seal the entrance.

Jesus commanded, "Take away the stone."

We all stepped back. Martha, who had been following Jesus and Mary was the one brave enough to say what we were all thinking. "Lord, he's been dead four days. By this time, he'll stink. He's decaying." What she meant, and we all knew she meant, was, "It's too late."

Jesus looked at her in pity and rebuke and said, "Martha, didn't I tell you that if you believed on Me, you would see the glory of God?"

She hung her head and then motioned to some men to take away the stone. When the stone was out of the way, the odor coming from the tomb was terrible. We all put our hands over our noses.

All except Jesus. He looked toward the heavens and prayed aloud, "Father, thank You that You hear Me. I know You always hear Me, but I say this for the people's benefit, so that they will believe that You sent me."

Then he put his hands to his mouth and shouted, "Lazarus! Come out!"

Everyone was silent. Waiting. Then I thought I heard a shuffling. Suddenly, a figure appeared at the doorway of the tomb, a body wrapped with the bandages used for burial and and his face covered with the customary napkin.

Time seemed to stop. I was astonished! I couldn't formulate a single thought. My mouth just hung open.

I did happen to notice that the stench of decay was gone. There was no more decay. There was no death in that tomb.

Jesus calmly said, like it was an everyday occurrence for him, "Untie him and let him go home."

Mary and Martha rushed to his side and tore off the grave clothes. Someone in the crowd gave Lazarus a cloak to cover himself with until he got home.

I heard many shouts of "Praise God! Hallelujah to the Almighty!" And it seemed that many of the crowd believed in Jesus now.

Thomas and Simon were flabbergasted like me. It was many minutes before I finally got my feet to work and take me back to Lazarus' house where we stayed that night with Mary and Martha and the man who had died but was now alive and sitting a few feet away.

I watched him eat and drink and talk. He couldn't answer any questions about the afterlife. He kept looking at Jesus, but Jesus would shake his head. That wasn't his job. Instead, he praised God and Jesus as God's prophet and the Messiah.

Maybe that Prophet would be the Messiah, as well.

CHAPTER 15 THE ENTRY

I noticed that some of the people who had been mumbling against Jesus before the miracle slipped away from the worshipers. They were headed towards Jerusalem.

We heard rumors that the dissenters went to snitch on Jesus to the Pharisees. They were bent on killing both him and Lazarus now.

I found that quite ironic, trying to kill the man who had already died and been brought to life once. What were they going to do, keep killing Lazarus until Jesus could no longer raise him from the dead again for some unknown reason?

The next morning, Jesus bade us leave before dawn so that we could go out to Ephraim near the wilderness. Was Jesus scared and wanting to hide from the Pharisees?

When I heard the scribes and Pharisees were offering money to anyone who could deliver Jesus to them, I must admit that I perked up.

The thought came to me that any money was better than none. Jesus hadn't delivered on any of his promises to me—or any of the twelve, for that matter. It had been over three years.

Father was likely out of money by now, probably even in debtors' prison. Not that he didn't deserve it. But Mother would've wanted me to prevent it if I could. She would have wanted me to help out Father.

Not that I cared. But what if my piece of land had been sold to another undeserving Judean and was no longer available?

I would be so upset if I didn't get anything out of these three years. Following Jesus was accomplishing none of this. I didn't want to have to betray my Master, but I really needed the money.

Wasn't it just good business to cut losses and quit anything that wasn't profitable, anything that didn't further my long-term strategy?

That's what I had learned from watching how my uncle sold Father's woven goods. It's too bad Father hadn't learned that lesson. But surely, my uncle would want me to put my business savvy to work.

I battled back and forth for a week.

After a week, Jesus set his face toward Jerusalem, hot spot for politics just then, with the beginning of the Passover Feast that week.

On the first day of the week, we went to the Mount of Olives with Jesus. He sent Philip and me into the village of Beth-phage to find a donkey. But not just any donkey. Jesus told us that we would find a donkey and her colt tied. We should untie them and bring them to him. If anyone questioned us, he told us to say, "The Lord needs them," and they would then allow us to take the donkeys.

I didn't believe that just telling someone that Jesus wanted something would be enough for them to just hand it over without any compensation.

But Philip acted like this was a perfectly normal request. Philip thrived on problem-solving and providing materials. He was an organizer, a planner.

So we went into the village, and there, just as he said, was a donkey with a foal. We untied them and were leading them away when the animals' owner barged out of the door.

"What do you think you're doing?"

We stopped, and Philip repeated the Master's words. "The Lord needs them."

I waited for him to say, "Yeah, right. I have no lord."

When the man's entire attitude changed and he said, "Oh, in that case, please take these donkeys for your Master's use," my jaw dropped open. I wondered if he were lying so he could find out who to clobber for thievery.

Though curious about Jesus' "prediction," I shrugged it off as wishful thinking. Boy, Jesus sure was lucky sometimes. I guess claiming the title of Messiah did bring a few advantages. At least we got the donkeys for free.

Philip and I brought the donkey and her foal to Jesus. Peter, James, and John spread their outer coats over the animals' backs and then helped Jesus get on and get comfortable.

By the time we were ready, most of the crowd had heard we were coming. Who am I kidding? They never cared about us. They only cared that Jesus was coming.

The crowd had spread overcoats and tree branches all along the road into Jerusalem, and most were shouting, "Hosanna to the Son of David! Blessed is he who comes in the name of the Lord! Hosanna in the highest! Hosanna!"

Those on the fringes kept asking, "Who is it? What's going on?"

And the people in front of them would call backward, "It's Jesus of Nazareth, the prophet from Galilee!"

I heard several exclamations of "Nazareth? Can anything good come for Nazareth?"

And the people in front of them would always answer, "Look! There's one!"

I laughed out loud at the looks on the faces of the Roman soldiers at the gate. They seemed worried that the crowd was getting loud and was shouting in Hebrew instead of Greek. Yet the celebrity, the man causing all the ruckus, was a peaceful man riding a sluggish donkey.

It was the least threatening display of political power I'd ever heard of. Maybe Jesus was trying to throw the Romans off his scent. That would have been a good strategy if I had believed his strategy was for the right goal.

Jesus may have set his face toward Jerusalem and unflinchingly made his way there. He may have planned a specific way to enter the capital city. But I still wasn't sure what his ultimate goal was.

It seemed he was publicly accepting the title of Messiah. This was the way the Messiah was prophesied to come. He had the support, or at least the popularity, with the common crowds.

He was coming as a king but not a conquering one. What else could he be planning to do?

By the time our slow donkey made it through the throngs of people into the city gates, it was already late.

Jesus went to visit the Temple but didn't do much except pray quietly in the corner for just a few minutes and then leave.

We stayed in Bethany with our good friends Mary and Martha and their brother back from the dead, Lazarus.

I kept waiting for his most avid supporters to ask him what was his next step to claim kingship. I kept waiting for him to explain his plan. But nobody had the guts to ask him, not even Peter. We were all wondering what this meant for us and for Israel's future. But we were afraid of Jesus' answer.

Now was the time to take advantage of the popularity and political fervor of the masses and use it to turn the tide toward real support for Jesus as Messiah. But Jesus didn't seem to want to do anything about it.

I was torn. I wanted to back a winner. But I also wanted him to want to win badly enough that he would work for it. Power wouldn't just be handed to him on a silver platter. If he thought that's what was going to happen, he was in for a rude awakening.

If nothing happened in the next couple of days, I would need to do something about it.

CHAPTER 16 THE ANOINTING

As I lagged behind the eleven, not wanting to be seen in Jesus' company if I could help it, a messenger boy ran up to Thomas and asked him if he was Judas, son of Iscariot.

Thomas gestured back to me. "No, but that's him."

He turned and trotted a few feet until I had caught up with him. "Judas Iscariot?"

"Yeah, what do you want?"

"I have a message for you from Brutus of Ptolemais. Here."

Brutus. Mother's master. What could he possibly want with me? Was she all right?

With trepidation, I hastily tore the Roman wax seal and unrolled the scroll. I read:

"Judas, son of Iscariot and Rachel. Your mother has done everything she can to win her freedom. But the council is demanding an extra fee of thirty silver pieces. I would happily pay it for her, but they refuse to accept it from me. It must be from someone else, another witness to her usefulness as a free citizen. If you can spare thirty pieces of silver, send them or bring them to me in Ptolemais. If not, I fear the council will refuse her request. I will continue to keep her safe and healthy under me. But if I should be replaced, who knows what will become of her. I am worried for her. For her sake, find a way to get the money here soon. Brutus."

The boy still stood waiting for my response.

"Can you stay a couple of days until I can get the money for your master?"

"Yes, sir. My master has specially ordered me to be of service to you either by bringing back the money or by showing you the way."

"Good. Meet me outside the Temple tomorrow at midday. I'll see what I can do."

"Yes, sir."

As he scampered off, I hurried to catch up with the others. They were headed back toward our friends' house in Bethany.

Martha had invited some of the leaders of the town to a dinner in Jesus' honor, which I wasn't happy about. Not that Jesus didn't deserve the honor. But I thought it was risky, especially not knowing whose side the other guests were on.

Everything was going fine throughout dinner. No heated discussions. No accusations. No traps laid in words. No hostility at all.

Then Mary had to go and ruin it all. She had been saving a very expensive box of spikenard, an aromatic oil from the Far East. She must have been saving it for her wedding.

It was a beautiful, valuable box. But she broke it at Jesus' feet, and sobbing, began to wipe the Master's feet with her hair, the oil spreading around her tears. The entire house was filled with the pleasant but almost overpowering aroma.

I couldn't believe she would waste such a valuable commodity! Even if she were thankful for her brother's return from the dead, it wasn't worth wasting it!

If she had wanted to give that expensive perfume to Jesus' ministry, she should have sold it and given us the money. Then I would have had a much easier time trying to ration out the food.

These fisherman didn't understand what resources were necessary to keep a traveling teacher with an entourage of twelve more men out of debtor's prison.

And I would have had the thirty pieces of silver to free my mother, for goodness' sake.

Nobody else tried to stop her, so I spoke up. "Why wasn't this valuable perfume sold and the money given to the poor? It was worth an entire year's wages!"

Jesus' looked over at me and shook his head, disappointed.

"Leave her alone," Jesus said quietly. "She has done a beautiful thing to me. This perfume was intended to be saved for my burial, which is happening very soon. You'll always have the poor among you, but I will not always be among you. Truly I tell you, wherever this news is preached throughout the world, what she has done will also be told, in memory of her valiant sacrifice."

Disgusted, I got up and put my sandals back on. I left the house without a word.

Outside I was surprised to see a large crowd who were trying to see a glimpse of Jesus through the doorway. I also heard many people asking about Lazarus, because they wanted to see a formerly dead man.

Then I noticed a handful of Pharisees and scribes clustered in their own group. The rest of the town was giving them a wide berth. But I heard them mention that Lazarus's resurrection had made so many people believe in Jesus that they plotted to have him arrested "at the very least."

I knew what more could be done.

CHAPTER 17 THE CLEANSING

The next day, Jesus led us back to the Temple. He wanted to spend more time there in prayer, I thought.

I was wrong. When we got there, he stopped in the outer courts and looked around at all the merchants and money changers and their booths of animals for sale as sacrifices.

His eyes flashed darker and darker, and his jaw clenched tighter and tighter, until he snapped. I had never seen him like this. His anger was terrible to behold!

He overturned tables, slid boxes of money to the ground, opened cages of animals, and even grabbed a whip and cracked it a few times. He never hurt anyone. He was just warning them. But boy, did he wreak havoc with the sacrificial system!

Simon the zealot and the Inner Three, as soon as they realized Jesus' intentions, began helping overthrow tables and setting animals loose. I just watched from the side.

Most of the merchants ran away, but several of them ran straight to the priests and Pharisees. A group of the chief priests marched up to Jesus, staying out of reach of the whip.

"What have you done, Jesus of Nazareth? You are a stranger and a guest in our city, and yet you presume to make this kind of spectacle? Who do you think you are?"

Jesus threw down the whip, threw up his arms, and called out passionately, "You have turned my Father's house into a house of selling, not of worshiping! As it written, 'My house will be called a house of prayer, but you've turned it into a den of thieves!' You will not corrupt my Father's holy dwelling place like this!"

"Your Father? Your Father!" The head Pharisee spat and sputtered. He didn't get any further, for Jesus had already turned and walked out.

From the looks of complete outrage on the religious leaders' faces, I knew Jesus had just sealed his fate. He had committed blasphemy and dared to assert his authority over theirs. This would not end well.

I knew then that an out-and-out war was coming. The Pharisees would not rest until Jesus was dead. Though Jesus would obviously fight for what he thought was right about religious practices, would he fight for his own authority?

The odds were highly in the Pharisees' favor. They had clout, connections with the Romans, and they had self-righteous fervor, believing themselves to be ridding Israel of a false prophet.

Even if Nicodemus and Joseph of Arimathea seemed sympathetic to our side, they wouldn't be enough to stem the tide of malice sweeping their ranks after this scene.

Jesus was going to die. And I'd be hanged if I went down with him.

CHAPTER 18 THE PLAN

I remembered my idea of cashing in on the Pharisees' attempts to arrest my Master. It was my last chance to free Mother.

I found the messenger boy and told him I thought I had a way to make the thirty pieces of silver, but he would need to wait for a few days. I would meet him again on Friday before the Passover began at sundown.

As I slipped away into the crowd of spectators, I felt as though I had no choice at this point. Everything was going to happen this way.

I didn't know where I was heading until I found myself outside of the Sanhedrin's meeting place, the Hall of Hewn Stones. I asked a guard if I could meet with the Pharisees. One of the most influential Pharisees, right-hand man to the Chief Priest, allowed me to come into a side chamber and present my business.

"I am called Judas Iscariot, and I'm one of the twelve chosen disciples of Jesus of Nazareth."

His beady eyes flashed in recognition of that name. But he remained silent.

I took a deep breath and continued, "I have talked with a Pharisee before. Do you keep in contact with the Pharisees in Capernaum? If so, they will have shared that I may have been under the mistaken impression that my Master would be the Messiah to rid Israel of these Gentile dogs, these Romans. But I was wrong. I see that now. He will never even try to overthrow the Romans."

His eyes squinted, and he folded his arms across his chest. "What makes you say that?"

"I've been watching and waiting. There have been many times that he could have risen in political power, or gained more popularity with the common people. Instead he deliberately chose words or actions that confused or angered his followers. He told several sinners he had healed to keep silent about the manner of their healing. The spectacle at the Temple this morning was the last straw. He will always be in opposition to your party, the honorable Pharisees. And he can never win against such a powerful, righteous group."

I bowed my head in flattery. Then I looked up again to gauge his reaction. He wasn't fooled by my flattery. His eyes were still suspicious. But they also reflected his interest.

"I have been in communication with our brothers in Galilee. They have told me of your offer. I also know they turned you down. Why?"

"They thought they could do it themselves. They thought they could handle Jesus and trap him by themselves so that they wouldn't have to pay anyone else to do it. The trouble is, they haven't been able to do it yet. You need me."

"What do you plan to do? What is it that you want from us?"

"I know for a fact that your people have tried to arrest Jesus and have even tried to stone him several times before this. Jesus has always somehow managed to escape. But what if someone on the inside, someone he trusts, were to help you surprise him? Once I know where he's going to be, I could sneak away and lead you to him."

He unfolded his arms and leaned towards me. "And what would induce you to betray your own Master?"

Ah, I had him. We were merely haggling over price now. Maybe now I could recoup some of that money I had lost by following Jesus for three and a half years, never getting anything for my sacrifices.

"Well, your money changers and merchants lost a lot of money at the Temple today." I slowly dangled the carrot in front of his nose. "Think of all the families who had planned to buy their Passover sacrifices today and were prevented from being atoned for their sins because they didn't have access to a spotless lamb or a perfect dove."

I reeled it in. "Think of all the common people whose faith in justice and the provision of the religious Pharisees is now shaken because of Jesus' assertion of his authority over you."

Now to move in for the kill. "What is that worth to you?"

A greedy light had shone in his eyes. He sat back and rubbed his beard. "A fair question. It would be worth much to us. However, it also should not be enough to be easily tracked back to us."

I made my offer. "Thirty pieces of silver is a bargain for this problem I'm going to solve for you. However, thirty pieces of silver would be a common denomination that no one would think to track back to its origins. I would be willing to do this deed for thirty pieces of silver. What do you say?"

I thrust my hand out, my heart pounding in my ears. The thrill of negotiation had not lessened. It was exhilarating to hold a man's future, a man's ministry, a man's life, in my own hands.

The Pharisee sniffed and then took my hand, shaking it firmly in agreement.

"Done. I will pay you when we have him in custody. How soon can you bring this to pass?"

"I don't know, sir. It depends on Jesus' agenda for tomorrow. As soon as I know where he plans to be, I will let you know. Sometimes we just seem to wander aimlessly through a town until he has healed everyone. Sometimes we march straight through. I don't know what his plans are in Jerusalem yet, but I know he's not aimless. He came with some purpose in mind. As soon as I find out where that will take place, I'll come and tell you."

"Very good. Don't wait too long, or I'll have reason to doubt your sincerity."

"Yes, sir. I understand."

"Oh, and make sure you watch for an opportunity to hand Jesus over to our temple guards when there's no crowd. We don't want to start a riot."

"Absolutely! Good idea, sir." I sauntered out, head held high from the invigorating feeling of winning. I began to whistle as I headed down the streets back towards Bethany.

But as I neared the house where my Master was laughing with his friends and my companions of the last three and a half years, my whistling stopped, and my feet slowed.

What had I just done? What would my Master think of me? What would really happen to him? The Jews had no authority to actually put someone to death. But that didn't stop the elite from accomplishing it somehow.

How could I ever look Jesus in the eyes again?

CHAPTER 19 THE SERVANT

On the day before the Passover, Jesus told us to get ready for the feast preparing us for this special holy day.

Since I was in charge of the money, I had to go along with the disciples in charge of haggling for the sacrifices and finding the right room and supplies.

There wasn't much haggling done, though, as everything had apparently already been planned. Jesus told us, "When you enter the city, you'll see a man carrying a water jug. Follow him to the house he enters and tell this to the owner of the house: 'The Teacher asks where is your guest room, so that he may eat the Passover there with his disciples.' He will show you a large room, already furnished. Make the necessary preparations there."

When we reached Jerusalem, everything happened exactly as he had said. The owner showed us the room, and all we had to do was buy the food for the Passover feast and explain to the servants how we wanted it cooked.

It all seemed very familiar, like acquiring the donkey colt just a few days before.

They really didn't need me there. The other disciples could have just taken the money and bought everything without me. But suddenly they took my treasurer responsibilities very seriously.

I had no chance to slip away from them to tell the Pharisees where Jesus was. At one point, I even felt paranoid enough to wonder if the disciples were deliberately keeping me under surveillance. What if they suspected something?

But I realized that probably wasn't the case. None of them were that smart.

Just after the food was brought out, we got comfortable in our customary reclining positions, all except Peter. He had connived to be seated at the end of the room, as far away from Jesus as possible. I think he was remembering Jesus' rebuke about being last to be first, and deliberately choosing the worst possible place.

If he was expecting to be called up closer to Jesus in honor, he was mistaken. I chuckled under my breath at his obvious disappointment.

I reveled in my own close position to Jesus. He had pointed me right next to John the beloved. He must have had no clue what I was planning. That would make it so much easier, right?

Unaccountably, my stomach tightened and my throat went dry. I left more on my plate than usual.

We had eaten almost all the food when Jesus got up. He quietly took a basin, filled it with water, took off his outer robe, and wrapped a towel around his waist.

Then he knelt in front of John and began to wash his grimy feet with the water and towel. Yuck! The feet were the nastiest, most unclean part of the body.

I couldn't believe it! This was our Master doing the work of the lowliest slave. Why in the world would he dishonor himself like that? Had he lost his mind?

No, he only wanted to use it as a very poignant object lesson. I will never forget it, so it was definitely effective.

After he finished drying John's feet, he turned to me. I didn't know what to say or where to look. Jesus was amazingly gentle. Well, I guess it wasn't very amazing. If I had thought about it, I would have expected him to be gentle. I had just never thought about it.

At one point, Jesus looked up into my eyes and seemed to be giving me a special message. I didn't understand what his eyes were trying to tell me, but I couldn't meet his gaze for long before the awkwardness and guilt made that too uncomfortable. I silently willed him to hurry on to the next disciple.

He seemed to take his time.

But eventually he went on to Thomas. Then James and Levi and Simon the Zealot. Peter was last. I guess he had had a lot of time to decide how he was going to react to the foot-washing, because as soon as Jesus reached for Peter's feet, Peter once again opened his big mouth.

"Master, are you going to wash my feet, too?"

Come on, Peter. It's not like your feet are any better than ours.

Jesus nodded and answered, "Yes. You don't realize what I'm doing now, but you'll understand later."

"Not so, Lord!" Peter scolded. "You will never wash my feet. We should be washing yours!"

Jesus sat back on his haunches and just gazed into Peter's eyes for a long moment.

He finally said, "If I don't wash you, you won't have any connection with me."

Peter's eyes opened wide. He threw up his arms, palms out, and bowed his head. "Okay, then, Master, wash not only my feet but also my hands and my head, too!"

Peter didn't see it, but the rest of us saw Jesus' lips lift in a quick smile of tolerance. Then he patted Peter on the knee and said, "Just your feet, Peter. The one who has already bathed doesn't need more than his feet washed but is completely clean."

He took the towel and began drying Peter's feet. He looked around the room and said to us all, "You are unstained, but not all of you." And as he said "not all," he glanced at me.

He did suspect me after all. I needed to act quickly. I tensed and anticipated an opportunity to escape.

After Jesus put aside the basin and towel, he put on his outer robe and returned to his seat next to John. He looked around, and we all waited for him to speak.

He asked, "Have you realized what I've done for you? You call me Teacher and Master, and this is right, because I am. So if I, your Master and Teacher, have washed your feet, then you also should wash each other's feet. I have demonstrated this to you so that you should do what I have done for you. Truly, truly, I say to you, no servant is greater than his master. Neither is an apostle greater than the One who sent him. Now that you are aware of these things, blessed are you if you do them."

I was struck by the echo of the first teaching I heard from him, the list of blessed people.

What is this blessed life he keeps talking about anyway? Why haven't I found happiness? I can be meek and humble, and I'm definitely poor. I hunger and thirst after righteousness, when it's profitable.

Weren't the patriarchs, our first fathers, mostly rich and blessed? Abraham, Isaac, Jacob, Job, King Solomon? They were all materially rewarded for their piety.

Was it that my piety didn't measure up to their standards? A twinge of guilt assaulted my heart. According to the law, I had never murdered, technically stolen, bowed down to idols, broken the Sabbath, committed adultery, or been a false witness in court. I deliberately skipped the commandments about taking the Lord's name in vain and coveting.

But according to Jesus' teachings, just to look on a woman with lust is the same as adultery. No man can say he hasn't lusted in his heart. But I've never acted on it. Surely, that counts for something.

And anger. According to Jesus' new law, just to hate a brother is the same as murdering him! I thought that was a little harsh. Just because you entertain yourself on boring days thinking of all the ways your enemies could die at your hand doesn't mean you're as guilty as a murderer with blood on his hands. If so, that's not fair. I want justice, not letting criminals go free to focus on the intents of the heart for crimes not even committed yet.

Blessed. Did it just mean wealthy? Happy? Honored?

I sure didn't have any of those things. Where was my reward?

CHAPTER 20 THE WARNING

I stared at my plate and played with my bread while lost in thought. My mind took in the bread and the herbs, every single item on my plate bursting with symbolism.

I remembered the few Passovers I could recall with Mother, when she made a big deal out of everything. Each food was picked up and taught about. Each symbol was explained to a young boy who didn't care about deeper meanings and who just wanted to fill his hungry belly.

I remembered both Mother and Father reciting the Exodus from Egypt, the story of the first Passover.

Father would start: "Tell all the congregation of Israel that on the tenth day of this month every man shall take a lamb according to their fathers' houses, a lamb for a household.... Your lamb shall be without blemish, a male a year old. You may take it from the sheep or from the goats, and you shall keep it until the fourteenth day of this month, when the whole assembly of the congregation of Israel shall kill their lambs at twilight."

Mother would take over: "Then they shall take some of the blood and put it on the two doorposts and the lintel of the houses in which they eat it. They shall eat the flesh that night, roasted on the fire; with unleavened bread and bitter herbs they shall eat it. Do not eat any of it raw or boiled in water, but roasted, its head with its legs and its inner parts. And you shall let none of it remain until the morning; anything that remains until the morning you shall burn.

"In this manner you shall eat it: with your belt fastened, your sandals on your feet, and your staff in your hand. And you shall eat it in haste. It is Adonai's Passover."

Father would continue: "For I will pass through the land of Egypt that night, and I will strike all the firstborn in the land of Egypt, both man and beast; and on all the gods of Egypt I will execute judgments: I am Adonai. The blood shall be a sign for you, on the houses where you are. And when I see the blood, I will pass over you, and no plague will befall you to destroy you, when I strike the land of Egypt."

Mother would continue in a sing-song tone from having memorized it so long ago: "This day shall be for you a memorial day, and you shall keep it as a feast to Adonai; throughout your generations, as a statute forever, you shall keep it as a feast. Seven days you shall eat unleavened bread. On the first day you shall remove leaven out of your houses, for if anyone eats what is leavened, from the first day until the seventh day, that person shall be cut off from Israel. On the first day you shall hold a holy assembly, and on the seventh day a holy assembly. No work shall be done on those days. But what everyone needs to eat, that alone may be prepared by you."

They would both finish in perfect unison: "And you shall observe the Feast of Unleavened Bread, for on this very day I brought your hosts out of the land of Egypt. Therefore you shall observe this day, throughout your generations, as a statute forever."

Then Mother would pass around the bowls of roasted lamb, herbs, and unleavened bread. And Mother and Father would pray and give thanks for that first Passover. All I wanted to do was eat, not wait for another long prayer.

But it was important to them to do everything right. After Mother was taken, Father still observed the Feast, but he would always take me over to a neighbor's house, and we would eat with them. They never did things as grand as Mother would have.

The feast had never been as special to me as it had been when Mother was there. But tonight seemed special in another way. Jesus had recited the entire passage from memory. And it would be forever etched in my memory as the night I would become a traitor.

When we had all eaten our fill of this special meal, not the tastiest by any means, but still rare enough to be a treat, Jesus leaned back and observed, "I have eagerly set my heart on eating this particular Passover meal with you twelve before I suffer."

At the beginning of the sentence, I felt a twinge of guilt. I was going to ruin what he had been anticipating.

Then I realized what his sentence had ended with. Again he talked about the suffering. I still didn't know what he was talking about. Could he know what I was planning?

Then he added something I still don't understand. "I will eat no more until my work for the kingdom of God is finished."

He reached for his wine cup, filled it up again, and said, "Pass it around, and share it with everyone." As we were pouring a little into each of our cups, he also reached for the leftover unleavened bread, more like cracker than the fluffy bread I liked, said a quick prayer of thanks, and broke it into many pieces. He passed each of us a bite.

I felt something solemn was going on, but I had no idea what.

Jesus held up a piece of bread. We all held ours up, too. I hoped I wasn't going to have to repeat a vow I had no intention of keeping.

"This is my body, which is given on your behalf. This do in remembrance of me."

When he put the piece in his mouth and began to chew, we all put our pieces in our mouths and began chewing. I wondered at his phrasing. How was dry, unleavened, broken bread like his body?

After we had all finished swallowing, he lifted his wine glass, and we all lifted ours. "This drink is my blood, a new covenant, which is being poured out and bestowed liberally." He lifted the cup and took a sip. We all took our sips.

Then he said, "But look! The Son of Man journeys has been set for him, but woe to the man who betrays him!"

The other disciples glanced at each other and asked, "Who could it be? Which of us would betray the Master?"

Fearful eyes and tense shoulders separated me from them. I knew who it would be. It was me.

If Jesus was trying to scare me into being a mere "yes man" and forgetting about all my dreams and expectations, he was so wrong. I threw up a wall and assumed a role.

When James turned to me and asked, "Who could betray him?" I shrugged and answered, "I don't know," with wide-eyed innocence. It seemed to fool him, for he turned to John and asked him the same thing.

Peter, from the other side of the room, waved to John and mouthed, "Ask him who is it?"

John, Jesus' best friend, the closest even of the loyal three, leaned back against Jesus and asked, "Lord, who is the betrayer?"

Thomas called out, "Is it me?"

Simon nodded and added, "Or is it me?"

Several others asked the same thing.

It would look weird if I didn't ask, too. "Master, am I the one?"

Jesus looked at me with those resigned eyes and said quietly, "You have said it."

My heart began pounding. Surely, the other disciples would catch on now. But they weren't paying attention to me. They were only worried about themselves.

Jesus broke eye contact, almost as if he were helping to take their attention off of me. The rest kept asking, "Is it me?"

Jesus held up his hands to silence them. He raised his voice and answered, "It is one of you, the one who dips his bread into the bowl with me." His eyes locked onto mine. "It would have been better if he had never even been born."

No one else caught it. I thought this would give me away. But no one else suspected me. Only the person I was about to betray. But his phrasing punched a sinking feeling into my gut.

'...Had never been born' reminded me of the scrolls I had heard read from the Teacher of Ecclesiastes, the Son of David. "And I declared that the dead, who had already died, are happier than the living, who are still alive. But better than both is the one who has never been born, who has not seen the evil that is done under the sun."

Was Jesus trying to say that what I planned to do was evil? So evil that it would have been better to have never been born than to do it?

I wrestled again with my conscience. I knew it wasn't right to betray a friend, someone who had trusted me to be a loyal follower. But he was the one who had promised me power and money, the ability to influence a new regime and not have to worry about my next meal.

If Jesus wasn't going to try to become the next king, then I would be out of a job. I would be forced to go back home to poverty and misery and admit defeat.

I refused to do that. Turning one gentle man over to the authorities was small beans in contrast to what I was trying to accomplish. For the nation of Israel, of course. Not just for me.

Our holy Scriptures, the God of Israel Himself, Adonai, had promised a Messiah to rule over all of Israel with a rod of peace. When was the last time our poor country had seen real peace? Sure, we didn't see many battles, but we were oppressed, slaves to the great Roman Empire and to Caesar, who blasphemed the name of God by calling Himself Divine!

My purpose was greater than one man. One man's life didn't compare to the entire nation of Israel, Adonai's chosen people. I was doing God a service.

But then my conscience pricked me and reminded me that Jesus said he was sent by God Himself. How could betraying this prophet of God be helping God?

The scene flashed in my memory of Jesus rebuking the Pharisees when he reasoned, "How can a house divided against itself stand? If you say I'm a son of Satan but I cast out demons, then how can Satan's kingdom stand?"

He was always the master of the rhetorical question. Of course it couldn't. If he had really been of Satan, he would not have wanted to cast out Satan's demons.

So the Pharisees were wrong about Jesus. He wasn't actively working against Adonai. Either Jesus was a liar or crazy or who he claimed to be. I'd already decided he wasn't a liar. No one could impugn his honesty, his integrity.

So he was either crazy or the Son of God. This was where I wavered. Could he really been the Son of God? And what did that mean? Aren't all of us Jews figurative children of God? What made Jesus so special as to identify as God's Son?

That seemed to imply that he thought of himself differently, higher than everyone else, which was crazy. He was just the son of a carpenter, a common man, who was rumored to have possibly been a bastard son of a woman who got pregnant before she and her husband were fully married.

He couldn't be the Son of God in any divine way. Some of his phrases and teachings seemed to imply that he was claiming equality with Adonai. That was either a blatant blasphemy or insanity.

I would be doing the people of Israel a favor to get a madman off the streets, especially one who had the ability to rile up the religious leaders like he did. Why, if I let Jesus continue, we might have a civil war on our hands. Simon the zealot might like that, but I sure wouldn't.

All this ran through my head in a few moments time. The other disciples were still asking who was going to betray him. Jesus looked around at them, and pointedly ignoring me this time, he said, "I'm telling you about the betrayal now before it even happens so that you will believe when it does happen that I am who I say I am."

It was almost like he had read my thoughts. Get out of my head, magician! Maybe that whole spiel about casting out demons was a ruse, a way to hide that he really was working on the side of witchcraft. He had known things that no one should be able to know.

Maybe he wasn't aware that he was working for Satan. Maybe he was just possessed and acting crazy. Though he didn't act violently like all the other possessed people I had seen in our ministry, I didn't have any other reason. No other explanation fit.

Jesus reached for another piece of bread and dipped it into the bowl. He passed the bowl to me. As soon as I took it, I knew he was giving me an opportunity.

"We will depart and go up to our special place in the garden of Gethsemane," announced Jesus, with a piercing glance at me. "Go," he told me. "Do what you're going to do."

I expected to be mobbed, that the other disciples wouldn't let me go without a fight, but nobody stood. Nobody seemed to care. Maybe they thought I had some business to take care of with the money bag. Whatever the simpletons thought, they let me go.

I ran. I ran right to the Pharisees.

CHAPTER 21 THE WAR WITHIN

The blood pounded in my ears, and the fire shooting through my side doubled me over before I reached the Temple Guard's meeting place.

I walked the rest of the way, hands pressed to my side and forcing deep breaths. The stars overhead twinkled just like any other clear night. But the twinkling seemed ominous somehow, like they were trying to tell me to run the other way.

I shook my head of fantasies and focused on the reality of my disappointed hopes. Maybe betraying Jesus to his enemies wasn't the best thing to do. But it was necessary before more unsuspecting Jews gave up everything to follow this supposed Messiah who wouldn't even persuade the masses to speak out against these Romans, much less stage a coup to overthrow them.

I was doing Israel a favor. The ends would justify my means, at least in this case. As long as it would benefit more than me, the act I was about to commit would eventually be seen as the good, preventative measure it was.

But the closer I got to the meeting place, the heavier my feet felt, and the less determined my will felt. I felt torn. But I mustn't let my emotions dictate my actions.

Logically, Jesus wasn't doing what he had promised, taking God's people and their land back from the Gentile dogs. Let's not forget that fact, Judas.

But I couldn't get the mental image of Jesus' gentle eyes out of my mind. Especially the compassion he had shown toward me, even as he had told me to go betray him!

Could I really do this? Could I really betray the master who had handpicked me to follow him as one of his elite followers?

Could I be known as the one who betrayed his own master and squander the fragile friendships I had forged with Thomas and Simon the zealot? Would they understand why I did what I did?

And was thirty pieces of silver really worth all of this? Thirty pieces were more than my father and I had been able to call our own in a long time. But in the grand scheme of things, what would it change? Father would just go gamble or drink it away anyway.

Though, why should I give it to him? It was my money. Thirty pieces of silver would be enough to free Mother and finally live happily again.

As I neared the dreaded meeting with the hateful Pharisees, I stopped in my tracks. Why did they hate Jesus so much? They were judges and guardians of truth and righteousness.

Though Jesus sometimes acted unpredictably, possibly even crazy, he was moral and good and upstanding and certainly loving. Maybe the Pharisees weren't as worried about righteousness as I had always thought and been taught.

I picked up my feet and pushed myself to continue my journey. My heart rode along in my heels, feeling each step on the dirt road like a hammer.

I had to dissuade the Pharisees from following through on their plan. I would refuse to help them after all. They wouldn't be happy, but I found that I really didn't care anymore.

Now with a purpose, my stride grew faster and more determined with each step. I neared the meeting place.

I walked up to the guard who asked, "What is your business here?"

"I am Judas, son of Iscariot. I have an appointment with Caiaphas' adviser."

"You are expected. Enter."

A man of few words. How refreshing. I had a feeling the rest of the evening would be filled with words. And not many of them encouraging.

I breezed past the guard with a fake sense of bravado. Inwardly, I wished I had never set foot in this building of unrighteousness.

The adviser motioned from his reclining position across the room and said in a condescending tone, "Come here, Judas."

As I neared the middle-aged Pharisee with an immaculate beard and fine linen robe, I breathed in the fragrance of incense. He was using the holy perfume to consecrate our plan of betrayal. How disgusting.

The righteous indignation I felt at this hypocrisy gave me boldness I don't know if I would otherwise have found.

"Thank you for seeing me, but I have found that I have made a terrible mistake. I won't be betraying Jesus of Nazareth to you after all."

His eyes gleamed with anger. "How dare you waste our time! You promised us the information to find your master. And you were promised a nice sum in return."

"Keep it. Thirty pieces of silver is not worth trading my soul."

"Your soul," he scoffed. "Your soul is not in question here. Merely your reputation. If you fail to deliver the Galilean, we will make sure everyone knows that you can't be trusted in business transactions. Your master will never be able to rely on you to keep the purse for his ministry again."

"That's fine with me." My bravado must have slipped as I imagined what would happen to me if Jesus refused to trust me again. This would not end well.

He smirked and beckoned me closer. I refused to move my feet.

"Be warned. Caiaphas won't look kindly on his plans being stalled. You can expect an excommunication from the Temple."

I gulped. If Jesus didn't forgive me, it wouldn't matter what a corrupt High Priest said to me. Hopefully, Adonai wouldn't pay attention to his machinations, either.

"You can tell your master that my master is not the hypocrite he is. He is much more forgiving than the High Priest. Perhaps you should be more afraid of his reaction than I should."

This stab hit the mark, and his eyes betrayed fear now. He reached for a glass of wine to calm his nerves, no doubt. What would Caiaphas do to him? I remembered how I felt under my father, and I pitied him.

"Come, let us both ask forgiveness of Adonai and forget this plan. Let Jesus alone. And let us leave Jerusalem in peace. That will be a great act of kindness that Adonai would approve."

He spewed out his sip of wine. "How dare you claim to know what Adonai would approve! My master is the High Priest, the most spiritual man in all of Israel! And we will still find Jesus of Nazareth, even if you won't help us."

I guess I hadn't made my point.

"But Jesus is not who you think he is. He's an innocent man just showing compassion to people who've never been loved before."

He scoffed. "Innocent? Why, I've heard him claim to be the Son of God! Since when is blasphemy innocent?"

"I don't know about that, but he has proven he is the true Messiah, the one Israel has been looking for, the one you must've been looking for, the one your High Priest has been looking for. He's proven it over and over in the signs and wonders, the healing, the prophecies fulfilled."

"Oh, really? And who are you to make this momentous decision, son of Iscariot, the gambler?"

Anger welled up in me. How dare he bring my father into this! But I took a deep breath and tried to use logic.

"The masses believe in him. If you arrest him, you might have a riot, a revolt on your hands. The Romans would not appreciate that."

He sneered and rang a small bell for a servant. I knew my time was limited.

I went for broke.

"But you're buddies with the Romans now, aren't you? The most spiritual man in Israel is cowing to the will of the Gentle Romans!"

As two burly Roman guards stepped to my side, the Pharisee nodded to them, and they grabbed my arms.

"You're proving it! Don't let your master make a mistake like I was about to! He'll forfeit Adonai's favor!"

As the guards pulled me out of the room, I called back over my shoulder, "My master was right. You're all hypocrites!"

I heard a fist being pounded onto the table and a low voice which might have been uttering a curse, though I couldn't understand the exact word. Good. Maybe I had finally gotten under his skin enough for him to heed my warning.

The guards pushed me out of the door. I sprawled in the dirt. Sitting up and brushing off my robe to their laughter, I began to wonder what to do next.

Though I dreaded the hurt and disappointment in his eyes, I knew I needed to tell Jesus that I had heeded his warning after all. I would beg to be forgiven. Would he let me continue to be his disciple? Or had I blown his trust?

I stood up and began jogging out of the city toward the Mount of Olives.

CHAPTER 22 FORGIVENESS

I hoped that I could find Jesus and the disciples. I knew the part of the garden near Gethsemane where Jesus had rested before. He must be there. He had to be there!

By the time I crossed the Kidron brook and reached the foot of the Mount of Olives, my side was shooting sharp pains up to my rib cage, and I was panting. Though used to walking long distances with Jesus and the other disciples, I wasn't used to hard sprinting.

At one point, I thought I heard footsteps behind me, but when I stopped, they stopped. I looked all around but didn't see anything. I must have been courting paranoia in my dread to face my Master.

I found the little path we had used before, and I walked toward my Master, both my salvation and my judge.

All I could think about was the pain I would undoubtedly see in his eyes. I know he already suspected me. He might think I was there to turn him over to the soldiers then.

But it didn't matter if he understood immediately or not. I just needed him to eventually forgive me. If he hated me for the rest of my life—which he would have every right to—I would want to kill myself. I don't think I could live with it.

My eyes searched in and out of the vines and olive trees that grew in abundance in that garden. Finally I saw evidence of life. Such as it was. Through the tree branches, I saw Peter, James, and John sleeping against some olive trunks.

But where was Jesus? Panic began to roil in my bowels. What if I had missed him? What if he had guessed my plan and he had left town and abandoned his disciples?

No, he would never do that. He must be around here somewhere. I took my fear in hand and pushed it down.

I snaked in and out of the trees, making my way towards the favorite three.

Then I heard his voice. That sweet, familiar, gentle voice. My fear fled. Jesus was here. But his voice sounded sorrowful.

He was talking to the sleeping disciples. He reached down and shook Peter's shoulder. "Oh, Simon Peter, are you asleep? Could you not watch one hour with me? Watch and pray that you may not enter into temptation. The spirit indeed is willing, but the flesh is weak."

How right he was! The Master was always right. How weak my flesh had been!

Before I could reach them, Jesus left and went about a stone's throw away from them and knelt on the ground. He bowed his head and began murmuring.

I couldn't make out what he was saying. But I had finally reached the three.

As John rubbed the sleep out of his eyes, Peter saw me first and grumbled tired, "So, you're back, huh? Where have you been?"

I didn't want to answer truthfully. They would likely know soon enough.

I just shrugged my shoulders and sat down on the other side of James, who asked if anyone had any water. When no one did, he harrumphed and got comfortable against his section of the huge trunk. Before long, I heard his snores.

I thought Jesus had told them to watch and pray. What were they supposed to be watching for? Soldiers? Apparently not me, because they didn't seem to care that I was there.

I peeked around the trunk and watched Jesus for a few moments. His head was almost down to the ground. He looked like he was either in pain or in grief.

I thought I heard a couple of words carried on the breeze, "Remove this cup from me. But not what I want, but what You want."

I knew he was praying to his Father. But what was this cup he was speaking of? And this was the first time I had heard him mention that he wanted anything different from the Father. But he still submitted his desires to the Father's ultimate will. What a great example of humility! This was why he was such a good leader.

Finally he got up and made his way back to us. I punched James in the shoulder to wake him up.

But Peter and John were still sleeping. Jesus, with sweat and what looked like blood dripping down into his beard, gently woke Peter and John again.

"You can rest later. Now is my hour upon me. Rise and let's go."

Now he turned to me and looked deep into my eyes.

I couldn't stand it. I ran to him and fell at his feet. I grabbed his legs and began sobbing.

"I'm so sorry, Master! I know you suspected me of treachery. I did. I went to the Pharisees. I bargained to trade you for thirty pieces of silver. A stupid trade. I should never have even thought of it! I'm so sorry, Lord and Master!" For now he truly was my Lord, too.

Peter, James, and John began cursing me and telling Jesus to cast me out. I knew I deserved it. But I knew Jesus was the only one who would forgive me, if anyone would.

He picked me up. The Master held me in his arms in a warm embrace. When my sobs finally abated, he pulled back just enough to look me in the eyes.

"You're forgiven, my friend. My Father and I forgive you."

I closed my eyes, choking back more sobs of happiness. I had cried enough. Now was the time to celebrate. I kissed his face and hugged his neck. I was forgiven! I belonged to him again!

Alas! I didn't know how short of a celebration I was to enjoy.

Before the three inner disciples could process my forgiveness, a band of soldiers marched up the path two by two.

"How did they find us?" I lamented.

Jesus looked at me with a strangely content expression and said, "They sent someone to follow you. When you didn't fulfill your end of the bargain, they knew you had betrayed them."

So I hadn't escaped from betrayal. I had just exchanged one betrayal for another. I was sorry that my actions still had consequences, but at least I had chosen the lesser of two betrayals.

Jesus patted my back, as if he agreed with my conclusion.

"It is time. Judas, I love you. Peter, I love you. James, I love you. John, I love you. Never doubt that. But now my time has come."

And the soldiers stopped in front of me and Jesus.

Jesus preempted the conversation. "Whom do you seek?"

"We seek the one called Jesus of Nazareth."

CHAPTER 23 THE ABANDON

T he chief priests and Pharisees that had tagged along now pushed their way through and held up their lanterns and torches to get a good look at Jesus' face.

His dirty, sweaty, bloody face was not attractive in this dark night with the light flickering from the torches.

But there could be no doubt that he was the one they were seeking to arrest.

Jesus admitted, "I am He."

He spoke the same words that were recorded in the second book of the Pentateuch, Exodus, in the Law of Moses. These were the very words that Adonai Himself uttered in the burning bush to Moses on the holy ground.

In that moment. I knew beyond a shadow of a doubt that He was who He said He was. He was the I AM. He is the always "is-ing One," "the One Who Always Is," the ever existing One.*

And all of us fell on the ground. I don't think the earth actually shook. But I could be wrong. There were several earth shakes in the next few days after that. But as soon as Jesus uttered this simple yet profound phrase, none of us could stand in His awesome presence.

As we all stood again, Jesus calmly asked, as though nothing strange had happened, "Whom do you seek?"

The soldiers looked at each other and at the chief priests. More hesitantly this time, one repeated, "Jesus of Nazareth."

Jesus answered, "I've already told you I am He. If I'm the one you seek, let these other men go."

Oh, loving Jesus! Even to the very end, He was still helping us, being our advocate, saving us.

It wasn't until this moment I thought about myself. I finally had time and mental energy to wonder what would happen to us, His followers. Would we be arrested, too? It was logical that they would assume we were all guilty of insurrection and traitorous to Rome.

Peter must have been thinking roughly the same thing, for he drew his sword and swung at Malchus, the high priest's servant.

Poor Peter. An uneducated fisherman had no reason before to wield a sword. Instead of severing a head from the body, he merely struck the servant's ear and cut it off. It was a nasty, bloody mess, but it wasn't a lethal blow.

Instead of striking fear into the enemy's hearts, it merely motivated the soldiers to draw their swords. And they looked way more intimidating than little Peter.

Jesus held His hand out to Peter. "Put your sword back in its scabbard, Peter. Shall I not drink this cup the Father has given me?"

Oh, so that was the cup He had been praying about! This was the cup, the circumstances He had asked the Father to take from Him if possible. I guess it hadn't been possible. For surely, if there were any other way, the Father wouldn't have allowed this to happen. And Jesus knew it. And He had surrendered to this chain of events. His peace was amazing to witness.

Jesus turned to the chief priests and Pharisees. He knew who the real culprits were. Thank the Father I had pulled away from association with them!

"Am I leading a rebellion that you come out to me with swords and clubs to capture me like a criminal?" Jesus raised His voice. "Every day I was with you, teaching in the synagogue and temple courts in public, and you didn't arrest me then. But let my disciples go. The Scriptures must be fulfilled in every detail."

The priest in front motioned with his head for us to go. I took a step backward.

Peter whispered, "But..."

Jesus nodded. The soldiers marched Jesus past where the rest of the disciples had fallen asleep waiting for them.

A very young man named John Mark had been in the Roman bathhouses late at night and had heard the soldiers talking about the chief priests needing them to arrest a blasphemer.

When John Mark heard this, he knew they were talking about Jesus and came to warn him just after I got there. When the soldiers pushed Jesus past them, another soldier made a grab for the nearest disciple, which happened to be John Mark. He pulled away, the outer garment he must have hastily thrown on falling to the ground. He fled with us, almost naked.

As we ran from the soldiers, I threw him my outer robe so that he could at least hide his physical humiliation. Nothing could ever cover our emotional humiliation at leaving our Master in His worst hour. Could we ever forgive each other for turning tail and running?

Could I ever forgive myself?

I followed the other disciples until we got to the foot of the mountain.

We all stopped, panting and asking each other, "What are we going to do now?"

Peter, shaking, mumbled, "He said we would abandon Him. He knew it. He said I would deny Him three times. I haven't done that at least. I must go with Him. I need to know what they're going to do with Him."

John laid a sympathetic hand on Peter's arm and said, "Come, we will both go. I have a cousin in the Sanhedrin. Maybe he can let us be with the Master."

When James made as if to follow, John put up his hand and said, "No, James, you and John Mark must go back to the Upper Room and wait. You'll be safe there."

James hesitated, then reluctantly nodded. John then turned his attention to me. Disgust flamed in every feature of his weather-beaten face. His eyes, the corners of his down-turned mouth, the tightness of his jaw and cheeks.

Maybe Jesus had forgiven me, but the rest of the disciples wouldn't be so quick to overlook my part in the arrest of their Master, likely leading to His death and to the destruction of all our hopes and plans.

John finally said, "Judas, the Master did forgive you before He was captured. I suppose that means you're still one of us. But don't expect us to like it."

It was more than I expected. I expected to be shunned and never allowed admittance into their group again. I nodded in relief and tried to explain away some of my guilt. "I am very sorry for what I did. I tried to stop the arrest and thought I had. I didn't know they sent someone to follow me."

"You should have thought of that before you left. But it's not my place to chide when the Master has already forgiven. You go with the others and stay with them."

We all nodded and briskly walked back the way we had come from the Upper Room. I hadn't taken this direct route, but the others had no problem backtracking.

When we all reached the Upper Room, James explained everything the others had missed, emphasizing my duplicity. I received many dark looks and the silent treatment. But I didn't really care.

All I could think about was my Master. What was happening to Him? Would they hold a fair trial first thing in the morning? Would they hold Him in prison indefinitely just to keep Him from His nomadic ministry?

I knew the Pharisees wanted Him dead. How were they planning to bring his execution about? The Jews were not permitted to carry out the death sentence without Rome's express approval.

Did the Roman officials have any reason to execute Him? What charges would they even try to bring against Him anyway?

He had broken some of the rules about the Sabbath, true. But was that really worth killing Him for, especially to the Romans?

I knew Pilate was trying to curry favor with the emperor. Would executing the Master help or hurt Pilate's relationship with Caesar?

So many questions swirled in my mind, barely landing before another one pushed it out and took its place.

My mind kept flitting from topic to topic. I remembered many words Jesus had taught.

For some reason, I kept remembering the ways he described himself.

"I am the Bread of Life." So did he mean that he was the staple to continue living? In what way? Maybe following him was the way to sustain spiritual life? Because James had recited what Jesus had said on the way to the garden:

"I am the Way, the Truth, and the Life." When James had told me he had said this, I had wondered what he had meant.

Did he mean that he was the way to Heaven? Or the way to an abundant life? Because he did mention that though the thief, and I assume that meant Satan, comes to steal, kill, and destroy, he came to give life more abundantly.

And then he also said he was the Truth. Not that he has truth but that he is the truth. Such a bold statement! That reminded me of another "I am" statement:

"I am the Light of the World." How is he the light? Or that he shined the light of truth on evil? Light exposes things, which I haven't always liked, I admit. But when it shows what needs to be changed so that we can change it, it's a good thing. Maybe that's one of the things his parables and teachings did was to shine the light on our sins.

"I am the Good Shepherd." A good shepherd does so much for his sheep. He leads them to green pastures, leads them to still waters, protects them from enemies, goes to find the lost sheep, uses his rod and staff to discipline and train them.

I was reminded of one of my favorite psalms. I hadn't liked memorizing much of the Scriptures, but this one had been easy and comforting.

"The Lord is my Shepherd, I shall not want. He makes me lie down in green pastures and leads me beside still waters. He restores my soul. He leads me in the paths of righteousness for his name's sake. Even though I walk through the valley of the shadow of death, I will not fear for he is with me. He prepares a feast for me in the presence of mine enemy. He anoints my head with oil, my cup spills over in abundance. His rod and staff comfort me. Surely goodness and mercy shall follow me all the days of my life, and I will dwell in the house of the Lord forever."

I always assumed the house of the Lord was the mighty Temple. But I realize that Solomon's Temple wasn't even built when David penned this. Did he mean only the Tabernacle? That didn't make sense, because he never actually lived there. He must be still talking metaphorically. Maybe the house of the Lord was figurative for a right relationship with Adonai. But how did one get to that point?

"I am the Sheep Gate." Oh, yeah. Jesus said he was not only the Shepherd but also the Gate. Maybe this was the meaning of "I am the Way..." Maybe he was saying he is the way through the spiritual "sheep gate" to get to rest and peace.

"I am the Resurrection and the Life." When he told Martha this one, I didn't understand. But then he resurrected Lazarus from definite death. His stink proved he had been truly dead. If he had the power to resurrect others, could he resurrect himself? I didn't think so. But it would be a wonderful miracle.

"I am the... Life." He mentioned that one twice. I wonder why it was so much more important that he made sure we knew he is life. If he came to show us the way to eternal life, I had missed it. Was it too late now?

And then when the soldiers came, he merely had said, "I AM," and no one had been able to stand against this truth!

What did this all mean?

Eventually, just before dawn, all of us disciples finally fell asleep, very uncomfortable, restless, nightmare-ridden sleep.

CHAPTER 24 THE CRUCIFIXION

Sometime before nine that next morning, Peter came banging on the door. While we breakfasted on Passover leftovers, he told us all he had seen.

The soldiers took the Master from the garden of Gethsemane to Caiaphas' house, the previous High Priest. Then they had taken him to Annas, the current High Priest, Caiaphas' son-in-law.

"While at the house of Caiaphas, John's cousin was able to get John close enough to watch the proceedings, though not to stand beside or talk to Jesus Himself. I elected to stay outside with the guard and servants around the fire to see if I could hear any unofficial news."

Yeah, right. He had just been scared, that's all. I couldn't blame him, though. I'd have probably done the same.

"The soldiers and servants told rumor after rumor about witnesses brought in to testify against Jesus but contradicting each other. I had listened and kept warm until a servant girl recognized me."

"She said, 'You were with Jesus of Nazareth, weren't you?'"

Peter shook his head and continued the story. "I just said, 'I don't know, and I don't even understand you.'"

He sighed and then said, "I walked over to the porch where I heard a rooster crow once. I didn't understand then. But then another servant girl began nudging those next to her and saying, 'This man was one of them.'"

I interrupted Peter's story. "So you admitted that you were a follower of Jesus, then, right?"

Peter looked at me with sad eyes. "No. I denied that, too. Then after a little longer, one of the guards walked close to me and then took a double-take. He said, 'You must be one of the Galileans, for your speech resembles theirs.'"

Tears began welling up in Peter's eyes when he told us of the curses he used to vow that he did not know this man.

We were all quiet, absorbing the story. I understood the guilt he was feeling. Was that the end of the story?

Peter drew a shaky breath and continued, "When the rooster crowed again, it jogged my memory. Do you remember when Jesus told me that I would deny him three times before the rooster crowed twice? How could I have forgotten tonight, the night when He needed me most?"

The agony in his raspy voice pierced my heart, his agony giving voice to mine.

"Once the memory of my final denial rushed in on me, I broke down and wept bitterly. The disgusted guards insisted I leave. I should have stood with Him and took His shame as my own. But I was a coward. I ran back here."

After some of the other disciples tried to comfort Peter, we waited for hours to hear news of either Jesus or John. Finally one of the servants of the owner of the Upper Room came to bring us water and bread, and we grilled him.

He told us of an uproar, many people gathering to see if Jesus would be released or be the one criminal who acted as the scapegoat, dying for all the people.

When he opened the door to go downstairs again, we all gasped at the sudden darkness. It was noon, and suddenly there was a darkness unlike any storm or eclipse I had ever seen. It was like the sun was covered, but when we looked out the windows, there weren't any clouds covering it.

I had heard my father deriding my grandfather about his story that he had seen the sun go dim. He had claimed that everyone around him had noticed it. He called it an eclipse. But it had only lasted a few minutes.

This was eerie. It lasted for three hours. My nerves steadily increased until I was on edge, starting at every little sound.

So much for going to the Temple to make our special Passover sacrifice. I was worried that Adonai would add this to my list of sins. I really needed to get to the Temple to offer sacrifices for my sins and be cleansed. I wanted to remain a part of the blessed nation of Israel, His chosen people.

But I was too scared of being recognized, especially by the Pharisee I had plotted with. And none of the other disciples were any more courageous.

We were all huddled in small groups of three or four, no comfort to be had in our common predicament. Instead, our fears fed off of each other's.

Then at three in the afternoon on the day of the Passover, an earthquake shook us off our feet. We heard screams and shouts outside. We huddled together wondering if the end of the world had come.

It might as well have.

I couldn't stand not knowing anymore. I jumped up and pushed past Peter. "I don't care if they arrest me, too. I just have to know what's happening. It's my fault anyway."

Peter tried to grab me, but I yanked my arm out of his grip and ran down the stairs. He didn't follow me.

I followed the crowd out of the city. I heard people screaming that they had seen dead spirits rise from the tombs. I didn't know what to think. Had everyone gone crazy?

When I passed the Temple, I heard people crying that the curtain separating the Holy of Holies from the rest of the Holy Place had been torn. And not just torn any old way. Torn from the top to the bottom.

Adonai, the God of Israel, was making a statement. What it meant, I had no idea yet. How could it be connected with Jesus? But if the torn curtain were true, then this was clearly a sign from Him.

I kept running until I passed through the city gate. There on a hill shaped like a skull were three crosses with bodies hanging on them.

I slowed to hopefully prevent the soldier's attention. They weren't paying attention. They were quaking as much as the ground had.

I scanned the audience and found John with Jesus' mother, Mary. They had their arms wrapped around each other and were crying. They were staring at the body of the middle criminal. As I looked at the mangled body, I could hardly even recognize a face.

I pushed my way through the crowd to them and asked John, "What happened? Who was that? Where's the Master?"

John looked up with tears streaming down his face and pointed to the middle cross.

"That was our Master. Jesus is dead."

The centurion at the foot of the cross fell to his knees and cried out, "Surely this man was the Son of God!"

I saw the Son of God dead. Jesus. The Christ. The Messiah. The One I thought would be our next king. I was wrong.

But at least He didn't die at my hands like He could have.

At that moment, it didn't matter that He had forgiven me.

My life was over. Jesus was gone.

CHAPTER 25 THE DEATH OF HOPES

John, Mary, and I watched as Joseph of Arimathea, a rich Pharisee, took Jesus' body from the soldiers and had it carried to his newly carved tomb.

I found it ironic that it wasn't until Jesus was dead that Joseph, who had been silent about believing in Jesus, finally gained the courage to stand up for his beliefs.

It registered in my brain. But I really couldn't react. I was numb. It was like I was a spectator, watching a play but not personally affected. I guess that's how my mind protected itself.

Without a blink or a nod or a sound, I listened to the women lament that they couldn't prepare his body properly for burial until after the Sabbath.

Mary Magdalene and the other Mary, the mother of James and Joseph, went to watch the soldiers roll a large stone in front of the tomb's entrance.

I know the women were just focusing on a little thing so that they didn't have to contemplate the meaning of the bigger thing. But it irritated me slightly.

All I could think about was the bigger thing, the implication of what had happened. And what hadn't.

I couldn't get the image of Jesus' disfigured face and bloody, naked body out of my mind. It was horrible, the stuff of nightmares.

I had seen some deaths before. I had even walked past some criminals being crucified before. But never had they been so unrecognizable, almost to the point of wondering if they were men after all, like with Jesus. If I hadn't known that only men were nailed to crosses, I might have wondered what kind of skinned animal had been tortured up there.

I couldn't shake my horror of the gore. I felt trapped in despair and hopelessness.

What good was Jesus' forgiveness if my actions still led to his death anyway? It was still all my fault. Maybe the Pharisees would have found some other way. But I had made it super easy for them.

What was I thinking? How could I have rationalized away my traitorous intentions in my mind?

After feeling numb for hours, I finally began to feel something. And it was worse than the numbness. I blessed my numbness. I prayed for it back.

Because what came next was far more painful. It wasn't just guilt for my wrong intentions. It was shame. Wave after wave of shame and self-loathing washed over me. I refused to eat. I refused to drink.

At first the other eleven left me alone. No one wanted to be near the man who had betrayed our Master. No one spoke to me.

But finally James picked up a bowl of bread and a cup of wine and sat down next to me.

When he handed me the bowl, I shook my head. When he tried to hand me the wine, I did the same.

"Judas," he began in an annoyed tone, "you have to eat. Whether anyone likes you or not, you've still got to eat."

"Do I? I'll just save some more for the rest of you. The rest of you can still go back to your old lives. I can't."

James squinted his eyes and watched me for several long moments. I just wanted him to leave.

Then he sighed and said, "I don't like you, either, Judas, but our Master did forgive you. That means something to me. It means He thought you were worth it. It means He thought you were valuable enough to be protected, just like the rest of us. It means He thought you deserved a second chance, just like us. We all left Him to His doom."

"Not all of us. John stayed with Him."

"Well, he went back to Him, yes. And he wasn't the only one who wanted to. But he ran at first, too. None of us were completely faithful to Him."

"But I was the traitor. It's all my fault."

"Yes, you were. It started out as all your fault."

"Gee, thanks for the encouragement."

"You're right. But who's to say the Pharisees wouldn't have found another way? You can sit here and wallow in misery all you want. But one fact remains. Jesus the Son of God forgave you. I don't think He would want you to waste this opportunity."

"Opportunity? What do we have left to look forward to? What could we possibly gain from this?" I asked. My anger masked my fear.

"Making good choices in the first place is better than messing up, for sure. But in the end, we all messed up, remember? There will still be consequences for sins and bad decisions. But repentance is still better than none."

I refused to look at him. He set the bowl and cup down on the floor and sighed. I watched him turn away out of the corner of my eye, but then he stopped and said over his shoulder,

"Eat and drink. Remember our Last Supper with the Lord. I'll give you a few hours to figure it out yourself."

CHAPTER 26 THE DOUBTERS

We slept in the Upper Room again that night. Whenever I allowed my mind to wonder about the future, the first thing it always brought forward was my fear of being crucified, too.

I sometimes fancied I heard knocks at the door. My heart would bang against my lungs while I envisioned Roman soldiers ready to knock the door down to arrest the followers of the "King of the Jews" so that we could suffer the same fate as our King.

That one day dragged on and on. That Sabbath, though we didn't do a single thing, was the least restful day of my life. It was the worst day of my entire life. Even worse than when the soldiers took my mother. This time I was at least partly to blame for the mess. Helpless. Nothing I could do. Hopeless. Nothing mattered anymore.

After the Sabbath ended on Saturday night, the women went out first thing on Sunday morning to see the tomb again. This was the first time they could walk outside the city, so they left just after dawn.

While we were waiting for the women to get back, we felt the ground shake again. It was even stronger than the first one on Friday when Jesus had died.

What could it mean this time?

After an hour or so, the door flew open. I held my breath, expecting the Romans. But the women rushed in, all trying to speak at the same time. Mary the mother of James, Joanna, and Salome had run to their sons and began explaining what had happened.

They were crying and laughing so much that I could only catch a word here and there: "Guess what? The stone... angel... soldiers... Jesus... gardener... risen!"

But Mary Magdalene took charge and called out, "Sisters! Let's talk one a time. Salome, you tell the disciples what we saw when we first arrived at the tomb."

Salome stepped back and began, "When we came to the tomb of Joseph of Arimathea, the stone had been rolled back away from the entrance, and a man in white robes was sitting on top of it. His face was like lightning, and his hair was as white as snow. It had to have been an angel."

Mary Magdalene interrupted. "Thank you, Salome. Joanna, you continue. What did the angel say?"

"Well, the guards were so terrified, that they fell down and stayed as still as dead men. We were terrified, too, but the angel told us, 'Do not be afraid, because I know you seek Jesus who had been crucified. He is not here, because He is risen, just as He said. Come here and see the place where he was laid.'"

Mary nodded at her to indicate her turn was over and turned to Mary, the mother of James. "Mary, you continue."

"Okay. We stepped up gingerly toward the opening in the cave. It was dark so we couldn't see much, but we could see that there was no body, just cloths laying around. Then the angel told us to go back here to you and tell His disciples that Jesus is risen and that He will meet you in Galilee. He especially told us to tell Peter and Judas that He would meet you in Galilee."

She nodded to Peter in sympathy and then to me, the distrust in her eyes palpable between me and everyone else in the room, except for James.

Then Mary Magdalene took charge again. She looked around at the disciples, the women, and the servants, and with an exultant and slightly belligerent stare said, "I have seen Jesus, our Messiah. I have seen Him with my own eyes. He is risen!"

She paused and dared us to contradict her. I merely looked at her in scorn. How dare she prey on our emotions just to make a more dramatic scene!

"The other women began walking back here. I stayed and looked into the tomb again. I began crying. I was thinking, 'What if this is just a big hoax?' The angel had disappeared from the stone. I also thought maybe we had all gone crazy."

She gave a smile to the women, silently asking forgiveness. They smiled and nodded. "We wondered if we were hallucinating, too."

Mary Magdalene continued. "As I stood there weeping, I looked into the tomb again and saw more angels, in white again. One angel was seated where the Lord's head had laid, and the other on the other end where His feet had been. They asked me why I was crying. I told them it was because someone had taken my Lord away and I didn't know where.

"I turned around and saw a man standing by the guards, who were still knocked unconscious or playing dead. I didn't realize who the man was at first. I thought he was a gardener. He also asked why I was crying and who I was looking for. I said, 'Sir, if it was you who carried away his body, please tell me where you took him so I can retrieve the body.'

"Then he looked me in the eyes and said my name. Just 'Mary,' that's all he said. But that's all he needed to say. He had spoken my name that same way dozens of times. It was Jesus! It was Him! He looked different and yet somewhat the same, but different enough that I didn't automatically recognize Him. Of course, I wasn't looking for Him in a live body, either."

The other women chuckled. I looked at the other disciples. Were they buying this outlandish story? Though Mary didn't seem drunk or crazy, she might be losing her mind slowly. It just didn't make any logical sense.

People didn't just rise from the dead. Okay, a few people did: Jairus' daughter, the widow of Nain's son, and, of course, Lazarus. But Jesus had done all those signs and wonders himself, as a prophet of Adonai with Adonai's power. How could a dead prophet raise himself?

I expected the other disciples to be as skeptical as I was. Thomas was, and so was Simon, though the zealot was waffling. I could see on his face the conflict between wanting to believe but needing a little more proof.

The other disciples displayed varying degrees of belief. James' and John's eyes began to light up with hope. Peter just gaped, his mouth open.

But Mary Magdalene wasn't finished. Her voice rang in the large room. "When I turned toward Him and called Him, 'Teacher,' He put out His hand to stop me. I was going to fling myself down at his feet, but He told me not to touch Him, because He had 'not yet ascended to the Father.' I'm not sure what He meant by that. But He also told me to go to you—and He called you His brothers— to tell you that He is ascending to the Father, 'to My Father and your Father, to My God and your God.' That's what he said. He especially wanted me to tell you, Peter."

Thomas then spoke up and argued, "How can you expect us to believe this story—that Jesus was dead and is now alive—on your word only? This is nonsense! What proof do you have?"

Mary was silent. Peter stood up. For once he didn't use his quick tongue. He just ran out of the door. I assumed he was going to the tomb to check out Mary's story.

John looked at James and then got up and ran after Peter. I called out, "Don't let yourselves get caught by the guards!"

But I don't know if he heard me.

We waited some more. I walked around and around the room. Several times I went to the door almost resolved to follow them and see with my own eyes, but then I would remember the guards. What if it were a trap and the soldiers were only faking?

So I stayed. We broke apart into little groups. Thomas, Simon, and I in one. Mary Magdalene talked quietly with James, Andrew, and Bartholomew in one group, and the other women excitedly chatted with the rest of the disciples.

Finally Peter and John returned. I was surprised at how relieved I was that even Peter hadn't been arrested. A few days ago I would have thought he deserved it. Now I was glad he didn't get what he deserved. Because I deserved even worse.

Peter began talking first, of course. He may have only been a fisherman, but he did know how to spin a tale.

"I ran to the tomb and saw the stone rolled away just like Mary and the other women said. I passed John..."

"But I beat him to the tomb," interrupted John. "Peter may have gotten a head start on me, but I still beat him," he boasted.

Peter shot him an annoyed glance. "Yeah, yeah, so you're in better shape. Anyway, though John got there first, he was too afraid to do more than just stand at the entrance. I ran right on inside the tomb. I saw the grave cloths, the strips of linen lying on the floor. I also the saw the napkin that had been wrapped around the Lord's head, still lying where the head had been but separated from the rest of the linen. Then John finally plucked up his bravery enough to come in with me."

John spoke up again. "That was enough to convince me. That was proof that Jesus is not dead anymore. The cloths were unwound like they would be if someone was taking them off from the inside. And the napkin was folded and laid right there where his head had been, folded like we fold a napkin at mealtimes signaling that we are finished. Remember what I told you Jesus cried, one of the last things He said on the Cross? He said, 'It is finished.' He has now completely finished His work. I believe God has done a mighty sign through Him, because He is truly the Son of God!"

I didn't know what to make of this testimony. If Peter's and John's words were to be taken as true, then the grave clothes seemed to indicate something strange had happened. It sure seemed like fact, because their stories corroborated, and they were at least two witnesses, not to mention the women. If the guards or the Pharisees or somebody else had wanted to move or steal the body, they wouldn't have unwrapped him first. That would have taken too much time.

Who would have stolen the body anyway? It couldn't have been the guards, because they were all unconscious or at least faking death. They wouldn't have wanted to appear weak or able to be overcome.

And it couldn't have been the Pharisees. Their whole defense was that Jesus was a blasphemer and their belief was that he was not the Son of God he claimed to be. They would have wanted to keep his body for proof that he was just a man, a rabble rouser. That's why they had hired the guards in the first place.

So who else would have wanted his body? I couldn't think of anyone. We, his disciples, had the most to gain from producing his body or destroying it so that it might look like something miraculous had happened. But all twelve of us had been in the Upper Room the entire time. I could vouch for every single of us.

And the women couldn't have moved the stone by themselves, neither would they have really had a motive to make this story up and look crazy.

I was at a loss. But there was really no proof either way. It was circumstantial evidence and hearsay both ways. None of this alone would be enough to prove this story of Jesus raising from the dead in a court.

I whispered to Thomas and Simon, "I wish this fairy tale were true. I really do. I just don't see how it could be possible. Wishful thinking doesn't make it real."

They agreed, and I felt vindicated. That is, until I looked at John's and Mary's faces. Though I still thought they were deluded or crazy, I envied their hope and trust.

CHAPTER 27 THE EMMAUS ROAD

Peter left that afternoon. He didn't tell anyone where he was going. Two of the other lesser disciples left to go to a village called Emmaus, which is about seven miles from Jerusalem. I didn't see who they were. I just saw their backs as they crept out the door.

The rest of us kept waiting. I began to wonder what our lives were going to look like day after day. Would we be stuck hiding in this Upper Room for the rest of our lives?

The owner of the house came to tell us the news. When the guards at Jesus' tomb reported to the Pharisees what had happened, they were dismissed but not fired or punished by flogging like usual.

"The rumor is that you disciples came by night and stole him away while the guards were asleep."

"That's outrageous!" Simon the zealot exclaimed.

James the son of Alphaeus, his brother, chimed in, "Yeah! How could we overpower a dozen Roman soldiers when we couldn't do more than cut off an ear at Jesus' arrest?"

"And if the soldiers were asleep," I added, trying to be the voice of logic in the middle of all these emotions, "then why weren't they flogged? Or worse? Something fishy is going on. And it's not the fishermen from Galilee. I'll bet the Pharisees are hushing up the guards with money. I should know."

I shouldn't have mentioned my involvement with the Pharisees, for I got some squinted eyes and dark looks. But I deserved them.

The owner reasserted himself. "I've seen more Pharisees hustling up and and down the roads than I ever remember! I think they're looking for any evidence of the body or of His disciples. You boys had better lock the door once I leave and only open it when I knock seven times. Got it?"

We nodded. It sounded like a logical precaution to me.

"But what about Peter?" asked John. He doesn't know the knock sequence."

"Well, if he hasn't already been arrested and makes it back here, ask him something only he would know. Okay, I'll come back in an hour with your supper and do the knock sequence."

Before the hour was up, we heard someone trying to open the door. "Who is it?" called James.

"It's me, Simon Peter. Come on, James, open the door."

"We have to make sure it's you and not the Pharisees trying to trick us. What did your mother-in-law say after Jesus healed her?"

Though the sound was muffled, we all heard Peter harrumph and then answer, "She said, 'Thank you, my Lord. It's a good thing Peter followed you after all.'"

James nodded and unlocked the door.

"It's about time." Peter looked exasperated.

Surely, he wouldn't begrudge us a little preventive caution, would he?

"I have something important to tell you," Peter announced as soon as James had closed and locked the door again.

"I have seen Jesus, our Lord and Master."

"What?" I asked. If these occurrences were true, why did everyone else get to see Him? Was He avoiding me because I had betrayed Him? But He said He had forgiven me.

John pushed past James to stand face-to-face with Peter. "What did the Lord say, Peter?"

"He told me He forgave me for denying Him. And then He told me to come back to you for the night. He said He had someone else to meet."

"Who?" Who else but us twelve would he want to meet? His mother maybe? Surely not his mocking brothers.

"I don't know. He didn't say. And then... He just disappeared. I know, it sounds crazy. But, one second He was in front of me, and the next, I was completely alone. I don't know what to think, except that He didn't look like a spirit or a ghost."

While we were still wondering about this story, the owner knocked seven times. James explained the password to Peter while he unlocked the door.

The owner brought in trays with bowls of porridge and loaves of bread. "Here is your supper, boys. Eat hearty. Also, I have two men here who want to see you. I recognized them as some of the other followers of Jesus. Should I let them in?"

We all looked to James. He nodded. "Very well. As long as you know they're not Pharisees."

"Oh, no. Definitely not. All right, I'll tell them to come up."

His feet clunked down the stairs as loud as a camel. Then we heard him loudly telling the men to "go on up."

I hoped we wouldn't regret James' decision to trust the garrulous owner.

The two men reached the top of the steps and walked through the open door. Yes, I recognized them. I didn't remember their names, but I knew they had been following Jesus for a while.

James put out a hand. "Well met, Cleopas. Well met, John Mark. Why did you want to see us?"

Oh, John Mark. No wonder he looked so familiar. He was the young man who had lost his cloak the night of Jesus' arrest and who I had given my cloak to. The same cloak hung over a baggy robe even now.

He turned to me and took the cloak off. "I believe this is yours, Judas. Thanks so much for the use of it. I thank you."

I nodded and took the cloak. I had never expected to see it again, though it was my only one. I was relieved to get it back. Who knew when I would need it?

Then Cleopas called for attention. "We have a story we need to tell you Twelve."

This sounded familiar. It couldn't be any stranger than Peter's story, could it?

"John Mark and I walked down to Emmaus today, as most of you know. We were discussing all of the things we have seen the past few days.

"As we walked and talked, a man walked up from behind us and asked, 'What are you talking about as you walk?'

"We stopped and looked down, sorrowful. I answered, 'Are you a visitor that doesn't know all the momentous things that have happened in Jerusalem these days?'

"He didn't act surprised at all. He merely asked, 'What things?'

"I answered, 'About Jesus of Nazareth! He was a prophet, powerful in both what he said and what he did, in the sight of God and of all the people. The religious leaders handed him over to the Romans to be put to death, and the Romans crucified him. But we had hoped that he was the Messiah, the one who was supposed to redeem all Israel.'

"When the man didn't say anything, I continued, 'And even more, it's the third day since he was crucified, and some of the women who followed him have amazed us with their testimony. They went to Jesus' tomb at first light this morning but didn't find his body. They told us they had seen angels who told them he was alive. And others of our companions went to the tomb and found everything just as the women had said, the guards unconscious, the stone rolled away, and the grave clothes in the otherwise empty tomb. No body. They did not find Jesus.'"

John Mark interrupted, "And then he looked at us and said, 'You're foolish and too slow to believe all that the prophets have spoken!

Didn't the Messiah need to suffer all these things and then to enter into his glory?' And he went back, starting with Moses and explained all the passages about the Messiah all the way up through the last Prophet."

Cleopas silenced him with a look and continued, "We had just reached Emmaus and the man asked us if we were going any further. We asked him to eat with us, for it was almost evening. When we sat down to the table, he took the bread, gave thanks, broke it, and handed it out to us."

Cleopas stopped and looked around dramatically, as if to make a point. I wasn't sure what the point was, though.

John got it, however. He guessed, "Was it the Lord?"

John Mark bobbed his head up and down. "Yes! Our eyes were then opened to recognize Him, and then He disappeared from our sight. And we asked each other, 'Weren't our hearts burning within us as He opened the Scriptures to us along the road?' We knew something was special about this Man, but we hadn't recognized Him. Like Mary Magdalene, He was like the Lord but not so much alike that we instantly knew Him."

James took control again and said, "We believe you that this was the Lord, our Master Jesus, raised from the dead. He has also appeared to Peter."

Peter repeated his story, and I noticed that not a detail had changed, which increased my belief that he at least believed it to be true and wasn't trying to invent a fantasy.

He emphasized the fact that Jesus just disappeared from his sight as well. That similarity between the two stories, unrehearsed, made me wonder if there was validity to their stories. I just didn't see how it was possible for someone to raise themselves from the dead.

Just before sundown, Thomas pulled me aside and whispered, "I don't buy all these stories, Judas. I'm going back home. I still have some clout with my family's business. Come with me, and we'll start over."

I hesitated. "What about my mother? She can come with us, right?"

"Most likely. At least come and have a look. Talk to my father, and see if there's a place for you and your mother. There's nothing for you to lose."

He was right. After all we had lost, there was nothing else anybody could take from us. The worst that could happen would be that it wouldn't work out, and I would have to go back home to Father with Mother. There were worse lives, I guess.

"Okay. Let's see if we can make this work. But what will we tell the others when we leave?"

"I've already thought of that. I'll say that Father needs an experienced weaver, and you agreed to come help my family."

I nodded. It should work. At least I hoped they wouldn't think that we were deserting them.

We walked to the doorway, where Peter, James, and John stood talking in low but animated voices.

Thomas inserted himself and announced, "My family has sent a message that they need me. And they also need an experienced weaver, so Judas is going to come help me. If you need us, you know how to find us."

I was surprised that he didn't even ask their permission. Eyebrows raised. But one by one, they began to nod their assent. James even patted me on the shoulder and said, "Safe travels."

A slight stab of guilt at our deceit plucked at my heart. But I was getting used to guilt.

CHAPTER 28 THE IMPOSSIBLE

We were only at Thomas' house for a few hours, when a messenger brought a scribbled note from Peter.

"We have seen the Lord! Come back to the Upper Room quickly!"

Thomas and I didn't know what to think. Should we risk getting caught on the way again?

We put off the decision until the next day, when we asked Thomas' father for advice.

He stroked his long beard and studied our faces in silence. Then he folded his arms over his chest and said, "You must find the truth. You will never be at peace here until you have proved or disproved this resurrection to your satisfaction. Go and find the truth."

When we returned to the Upper Room, we knocked seven times for the correct password. James let us in, and his pursed lips, raised eyebrows, and wide eyes alerted me that something momentous must have happened.

I looked around and counted all the disciples to see if one of them had been captured. But they were all accounted for.

James said, "We have all seen the Lord now! I'm sorry you two missed it. Just after you left, we were still talking about the appearances to Mary Magdalene, Peter, and Cleopas and John Mark, and suddenly Jesus Himself was in the middle of us! Right here!" He pointed to the spot. "And He said, 'Peace be with you.'"

"Yeah, we were all terrified," chimed in Simon the zealot. "We thought at first that He was a ghost."

Then John, with a radiant light shining from his eyes, said, "But He told us not to be troubled. He asked, 'Why are doubts rising in your minds? Here, look at my hands, and look at my feet. It's me! Touch me and see for yourselves. A ghost doesn't have flesh and bones like I have.' And we felt his hands, even the nail prints still in his wrists, and in his feet."

James nodded and continued, "That's right. I felt them myself. And while we could barely believe because of our amazement and joy, He asked for something to eat and then ate it right in front of us to show us He was alive. He told us, 'This is what I told you while I was with you, if you remember. Everything that has happened has been in fulfillment of the prophecies, and those things still to come that are written about me in the Law of Moses and in the Prophets must be fulfilled, too.'"

Peter asserted himself and added, "And then He also breathed on us. He said, 'Peace be with you! As the Father has sent me, I am sending you now. Receive the Holy Spirit.' And then He disappeared again."

Thomas and I looked at each other. I wanted to believe. I really did. I wanted the consequences of my betrayal to be reversed. But why did I keep missing the "appearances"? It didn't sound like Jesus to deliberately avoid me.

Thomas cleared his throat and said, "I'm sorry, my brothers, but I cannot accept this on your word alone. Until I can see the nail prints in his hands and put my hand into the spear mark on his side, I can't believe that it's really him and not just your wishful thinking, or some deception."

I nodded reluctantly. "I must agree with Thomas. There have been four so-called sightings now, and I've not seen anything. There has been no physical evidence that I have seen with my own eyes. Without evidence, I'm afraid I can't quite submit to this absurd story."

The others stared at us with hanging jaws. Then sorrowful eyes replaced the astonishment.

"Just wait until you see."

O ne week after the other disciples saw him, after the next Sabbath, we were all in the Upper Room still. We had heard that the Pharisees had escalated their efforts to find us. We hoped the fervor would die down enough for us to sneak away. But it wasn't time yet.

The door was still locked, and the owner still used the secret password.

Suddenly, there stood Jesus. The door remained shut and locked. He just... appeared.

We all started and gasped. He said comfortingly, "Peace be with you!"

As my brain began to adjust to this miracle, he turned to Thomas and me and said, "Here, touch my hands, feel the scars in my hands and side. Stop doubting and believe now."

Thomas and I hesitantly put out our hands. When I touched his hand, a shock went through my body. It felt like he had always felt. It was a solid body, not like a ghost. And He was most definitely real.

Thomas fell to his knees and cried, "My Lord and my God!"

Then it suddenly clicked for me. The way Jesus could raise from the dead was because He was God Himself! The Son of God was equal with God because He is God! I fell down beside Thomas and grabbed Jesus' foot. I couldn't think of anything else to say, so I repeated Thomas's declaration.

"My Lord, and my God!"

Jesus put a hand on each of our heads and blessed us. He smiled compassionately and said, "You have believed because you have seen me. But blessed are those who believe even though they don't see me."

"Yes, Lord. We believe. Help our unbelief." The words of the demon-possessed boy's father came back to my memory, and fit just as well.

"Now get ready to go into Galilee. I will make a way for you to escape the Pharisees and meet me by the Sea of Galilee. Goodbye for now, my friends."

And He disappeared. Just like that, He was gone again.

CHAPTER 29 THE BREAKFAST

The next morning, with the help of the owner, we escaped Jerusalem somehow and began our journey to Galilee.

Because Jesus had told us that He would be going ahead into Galilee, we all agreed that we should follow.

When we arrived, we didn't know where to go. We stayed at Peter's house the first night, but it was really crowded.

Peter, James, John, Nathanael from Cana, Thomas, Simon the zealot, and I were all walking along the shore, looking for Jesus. I half expected Him to come walking on the water again.

But He wasn't there.

After hours of waiting. Peter, in a bored tone, declared, "Well, I need to be doing something. I'm going to go fishing."

We all said, "We'll go with you."

So James, John, and Peter bartered for a boat big enough to hold us. We went out into the boat and fished and fished.

We fished all night. A few of us dozed, and then we would wake and the others would doze. Someone was always fishing. But no one caught a single fish.

I wasn't surprised that I didn't catch any. I had never been fishing in my life. I wasn't impressed with the boredom, either.

We tried different lures, different baits, different depths, different sides of the lake. It didn't matter. We didn't even get a nibble. Not any of us.

By morning, we were all tired and grumpy. So much for going back to the old life. So much for the fishermen financing the ministry by doing what they were supposed to be doing best.

We headed back to the shore where we had rented the boat. Too bad Peter's boat had been confiscated. And John and Jame's father, Zebedee, was no where to be found.

A man waited for us at the shore. At first I thought it must be the renter, impatient for his precious boat to be returned, but the figure was taller and thinner than the rotund renter.

As we got closer and closer, he remained still. When we got close enough, he shouted out to us, "Friends, haven't you caught any fish?"

"No," Peter and James answered.

"Then throw your net on the right side of the boat, and you'll find some there."

I scoffed. "Please. We already tried everything. We just tried that side. What makes him think we'll get any fish this close to land?"

John said, "I feel that we should do as he says. There's something about this man."

Peter looked at him and shrugged. He and John let down the nets on the right side. Was that the starboard side? I could never remember.

Suddenly, the boat lurched to that side. Peter and John's arms were almost wrenched out of their sockets. "Help! The net's so full, we can't lift it!"

James and Nathanael sprang to help, but they still couldn't pull the net in.

John straightened, his eyes wide with amazement, recognition, and joy. He cried, "It's the Lord!"

Something snapped in my mind, too. Oh, yeah, the fishermen had told of their very first meeting with the Lord when the same thing had happened. That's when He had called them "fishers of men."

Peter straightened, looked at John, looked at the shore, threw off his outer robe, and jumped out of the boat. He swam for just a bit until he could stand. We weren't far from shore, only about a hundred yards or so.

The rest of us rowed toward shore, towing the net over the side until we couldn't row anymore. Nathanael and James jumped out and helped pull the boat in the rest of the way.

We looked around for Peter. We saw a fire pit on top of a rise, with Jesus and Peter sitting around it, already cooking fish over the coals. As we neared, I could see they also had some bread. Where did all this come from in such a short time?

Had Jesus planned this all along? Or had He miraculously provided the food again?

Jesus called out, "Bring some more of the fish you've just caught."

Peter walked back with John and climbed back into the boat, dragging the net all the way up to the shore. It was full of fish. Later, when they counted, they counted 153 large fish. Even with so many huge fish, the net wasn't torn at all.

When they brought an armload of fish each, I moved upwind. I was not used to the stink at all.

Jesus stood and held out his arms. "Welcome! Have some breakfast."

By this time, we were all sure it was the Lord. We didn't have to ask who it was.

Jesus sat down, took the bread, broke it into pieces, and handed each of us a piece. It was so like every other meal I remember. Like the feeding of the 5,000 men. Like the 4,000. Like the Last Supper we had with Him. It was at that Last Supper He had warned me, "It would have been better if that man who betrayed me would never have been born."

My eyes began to get hot, and my throat felt dry. I cleared it and rubbed my eyes, as He broke the fish and gave thanks for the meal.

He looked at me with such compassion in His brown eyes!

"I told you already that I have forgiven you, Judas. There's no need to condemn yourself. I have wiped your sin clean. Only believe, go out, and sin no more."

I nodded. "Yes, Lord. I will do whatever You say."

We ate in companionable silence, basking in Jesus' smiles and in His presence. It was just like it had always been.

When we finished eating, Jesus turned to Peter and called him by his old name. "Simon, son of John, do you agape me more than these?" He gestured to the fish still in the net.

"Yes, Lord," Peter answered, nodding. "You know that I phileo You."

I tilted my head toward Peter. He didn't exactly answer the question.

But Jesus didn't call him out on that. He merely answered, "Then feed my little lambs."

I wasn't sure what Jesus was trying to say here. If Peter loved him more than fish, he was supposed to become a shepherd now?

After a few moments, Jesus asked again, "Simon, son of John, do you agape me?"

Peter hesitated, then answered just as before, "Yes, Lord, you know that I phileo You."

He still didn't answer the question. Couldn't he see that Jesus was looking for another answer? All he needed to say was, "Yes, I agape You." That's all. Couldn't Peter even get that simple question right?

Jesus answered, "Shepherd my sheep."

I almost missed it. The first time Jesus had said "little lambs." Now He said "sheep." And this time He had changed the verb. The first was "feed," but this time it was "shepherd." What did He mean?

Again, Jesus's gaze bored into Peter and asked, "Simon, son of John, do you phileo me?"

Peter looked hurt because Jesus used his old name, not the new name He had given him. And He asked him yet again, even though Peter had told Him twice that he did phileo Him.

I could have told Peter it was because Jesus was looking for a particular answer, but I kept my mouth shut. Peter needed to figure this out on his own. And I also figured that Jesus didn't need help teaching His own lesson.

Jesus glanced at me with an approving look. Did He know what I was thinking? He nodded almost imperceptibly. I guess so.

Peter cried, "Lord, You know all things. You know I phileo You."

Ah, so Peter wouldn't say agape if he didn't think he was being honest. Good job, Peter. Maybe you are learning.

This time Jesus answered, "Then feed my sheep." I wished Jesus would explain what He meant, for it was obviously important, at least to Peter, because He repeated it three times. He always repeated what He wanted us to remember.

This time, Jesus continued, "Truly, truly I say to you that when you were younger, you dressed yourselves and went where you wanted to go. But when you are old, you will stretch out your hands, and someone else will stretch out your hands for you, and someone else will lead you where you do not want to go."

All the rest of us looked at each other and shrugged our shoulders. This sounded like a prophecy for Peter's future, but we had no idea what it meant. Where would he not want to go?

Then Jesus added, "Follow me!"

It reminded me so much of the very first day I had met Jesus. When He had looked directly at me, seeming to see right through me, probably knowing what kind of thieving scoundrel I had been, and yet He had asked me to follow Him anyway.

After what I had done to Him, though He had forgiven me, I still wanted to make up for it. I was glad Jesus hadn't asked me that question. I don't know how I would have responded honestly, either.

But I did want to show Him that I appreciated His forgiveness. I would follow Him anywhere still.

Peter, though, seemed to miss the opportunity to pledge His loyalty to Jesus. He looked around at all of us and especially at John. He knew that John had a specially close relationship with Jesus. If Jesus was asking Peter to follow Him again, wouldn't He ask John, too?

Peter turned back to Jesus and asked, "What about him, Lord?"

Was he jealous?

Jesus didn't even look at John. He smiled a little sadly and answered, "Even if I wanted him to remain with me until my kingdom comes, what is that to you? Don't worry about him. You follow me."

We all fell to our knees one by one and pledged, "I will follow You until death, Lord."

"Now, I would like to speak with Judas alone," commanded Jesus.

I gulped. Surely I wasn't in trouble. Was I? I replayed the conversation in my mind, trying to remember if I had thought something unlawful. After a lifetime of letting my thoughts have full reign in my mind and heart, I'm sure it would take me a long time to purge that habit. But surely Jesus would understand that and give me kudos for trying.

The other disciples' faces showed that they, too, believed I would receive a rebuke. It was also easy to see that some of them still hadn't forgiven me, because they smirked like they were happy I was going to get scolded.

"Yes, Lord? What have I done wrong now?" Let's get this over with.

Jesus' warm smile lit up my heart. It wasn't condemning at all. Even if I did deserve it. "You have no need to fear me, Judas. You will face the consequences of your previous actions, and the others will distrust you for awhile longer. But you just focus on Me. I want you to learn humility and support Peter, James, and John as the head of my new church. But that doesn't mean you don't have a very important role to play, as well. Will you do that for me, Judas? Learn to follow the under-shepherds that I as Your Good Shepherd have placed over you?"

"Yes, Lord. Humiliation was always thrust upon me, but I'm afraid I've never had a very humble heart. I will endeavor to do my best."

"You will have help soon. I will be leaving the Earth soon so that my Spirit, the Comforter, can come and dwell with you. All of you. Wait patiently in Jerusalem for the Spirit to come, and then you all will be My witnesses unto all the world."

"Yes, Lord. I will do all You say. You are my Lord."

He laid His hand on my head and blessed me. Then He was gone again.

CHAPTER 30 THE MESSENGER

Right in the middle of thanking God for forgiveness and restoration one day soon after Jesus' Ascension, I remembered the boy waiting for me at the Temple.

Oh, no! I forgot all about getting the money to him for Mother's freedom!

Now what am I going to do? I don't have any other means of making money.

And now that Jesus is risen from the dead, it doesn't seem to matter as much. Whatever else may happen, we are supposed to wait in Jerusalem for the coming of the Holy Spirit. I don't want to miss that.

And in all honesty, I'm not going to worry about settling down on my land. It's no longer important to establish a new name for myself. I don't care if anybody knows my name—whether from my father's ill reputation or whether from establishing a new reputation.

I do still want to spend time with Mother, but that may not happen. Besides, if she's still set on going back to Father, then she wouldn't need a house with me.

The only thing I worry about is buying her freedom in the first place. Maybe Brutus could find someone else to be a benefactor. Yahweh would protect her and watch over her. Jesus, the I AM, would not leave or forsake her, just like He stayed with me.

I told James that I had a messenger waiting for me at the Temple.

He raised both eyebrows. "What kind of messenger?"

A twinge pierced my heart. He still suspected me of treachery. I guess I brought it on myself. Still, James had been the first to forgive me after Jesus.

"A boy from my mother's slave-owner. He's been waiting for me since the day Jesus was crucified. If he's still there, I need to get a message to Mother that I won't be able to help buy her freedom after all."

Comprehension and then compassion washed over his face. "Oh, so that's why you needed the money? To free your mother?"

I nodded.

James studied me for another long moment and then said, "Very well. You can go. But be careful that none of the priests or Romans see you, or you could suffer the same fate as our Master—without the miracle."

"I understand. I will be careful."

"And don't let them follow you back to us, either. You might want to take the scenic route."

I nodded. That seemed reasonable. And I owed everyone there my best effort at protection.

"If anyone tries to follow me, I'll lose them. Don't worry. I won't betray any of you. I promise."

That was all I could do. Would it be enough to earn James' trust?

He finally nodded. "Go. Be safe."

"Thank you."

I headed out the house, glancing from one side of the street to the other. No Roman guards at the moment.

I pulled the hood on my cloak over my head and stepped into the flow of travelers toward the center of town and the Temple. It was easy to blend in.

As I neared the Temple, though, I saw more soldiers and scribes. Any one of them could recognize me. I stayed huddled in the middle of the traffic, thinking that it should be easier to stay unnoticed.

Now where was that messenger boy? Had he tired of waiting and gone back to Brutus already? Could I trust him not to rat me out to the Pharisees?

I scanned the outer court and noticed a short boy leaning against one of the money changers' tables, eating some dates. Was that him?

I maneuvered through the crowd to the tables. Looks like the money changers hadn't heeded Jesus' warning. They had returned to their previous schemes and scams.

I appeared to browse the man's pigeons and covertly scanned the boy's face. Yes, it was the same lad. Now how to convey the necessity of keeping my identity secret.

"Hey, there, boy. Where did you get those good-looking dates?"

He peered up at me and recognized me. I put a finger to my lips quickly and then pretended to need to scratch my nose.

He nodded slightly.

Good. He was intelligent.

He looked at the date in his sticky palm and answered, "I found a grove just outside the city that the farmer said I could eat from anytime."

"Would you show me this farm? I might have a business proposal for him."

He nodded vigorously, his eyes shining. "Sure, mister. It's this way."

I followed him out of the Temple square and into a dark alley. When we were sure we were alone, I asked him if he could still take a message to Brutus.

He said, "Sure. I need to get back soon, though. Where's the money?"

I hung my head. "I didn't get it. My plan backfired, thankfully, and I don't have any other way to earn money right now."

"'Thankfully?' How can you be glad your plan didn't work?" He raised an eyebrow.

He must think me crazy. I smiled sadly. "I made a bad decision. If my plan had succeeded, I would have betrayed a trusted friend, my Master, to his death. Thankfully, it didn't work out quite like that. But

I also didn't earn the blood money, so I'm hiding from the leaders and can't make any more money."

"Oh! Are you one of those Galileans everyone was talking about? Jesus of Nazareth's disciples, right?"

"Yes, but you can't say anything to anyone." I glanced around to be sure of our solitude. "You will have to go back to Brutus and tell him I won't be able to free my mother like I had planned. Tell him I will help as soon as I can, but I have no idea when that will be. Ask him if he can find another benefactor to take my place. And ask him to give my mother my love."

My throat caught as I realized I might not ever get to tell Mother that I love her again. As long as Brutus cared about her, though, he would make sure she was safe and sheltered. The rest would have to be left up to Adonai.

"All right, mister. I'll tell them all that. He won't be happy, though."

"I'm sure. I'm not happy about it, either. But it's part of the consequences for my intentions. I know that Adonai will keep watch over her."

He tipped his head and slit his eyes. "You Jews sure have a funny religion. You pray to Adonai and then give the Romans innocent men to crucify for Caesar. I don't understand you. Or the Romans, for that matter. Thank goodness, I'll never be one of them. Or you."

"You should be proud to be who you are, of course. But anyone can believe in Adonai, the God of Abraham, Isaac, and Jacob. The Holy Scriptures predicted that a Messiah, an anointed King, would come just as Jesus did. Most of the Jews didn't want to believe that He was their king, the Son of God. But He was. He is. I've seen Him risen from the dead."

He scoffed and turned away. I grabbed his shoulder, careful to be gentle. "Don't dismiss Jesus the Christ so quickly. I've touched His scarred hands and His pierced side. I know it sounds fantastic, but it's the truth. And I'm not the only eye-witness. Think about these things, boy. Your eternal life could depend on it. Ask my Mother when you get back. She can tell you all about Adonai."

He shrugged, and I released his shoulder. "Fine, mister. Whatever. Just let me go back to Brutus. At least he's sane."

He laughed as he ran off. I let him go. He was no longer my concern, though I would add him to my prayers, along with Brutus and Mother.

CHAPTER 31 THE COMMISSION

In those forty days after Jesus' resurrection, He appeared to us many times, and to many other people, too. Besides us Twelve and the women who ministered to Him, I believe there were over 500 people at one time who saw Jesus the Messiah, the Son of God, since He died, was buried, and rose again on the third day.

This was a time of joy, amazement, and rest. Jesus didn't want us to do anything yet, only to soak up what He taught us and showed us. One day when He had been eating with us, He specifically told us to stay in Jerusalem and wait for the gift of the Holy Spirit.

There were times I wanted to get out and tell the world, but I knew He had a plan and that this wasn't the right time. It was hard to wait sometimes. But we all needed a spiritual, emotional, and physical rest. I had a feeling it was in preparation for something big. It was hard to be patient.

Then, on the fortieth day, He told us to meet Him on the Mount of Olives. We climbed all the way to the top. There He appeared to us again. We bowed down and worshiped Him for a while.

Then He began instructing us. "All authority is given to me both in Heaven and on Earth. I therefore charge you to go in my name and make disciples of all nations, baptizing them in the name of the Father, the Son, and the Holy Spirit, and teaching them to keep all that I have commanded you. And look, pay attention: I am with you always, even until the final time."

When He paused, we gathered in closer. Peter asked, "Lord, is this the time you're going to restore the kingdom of Israel?"

I'm sure we had all wondered that. But I knew in my heart that this was not Jesus' goal. The kingdom of God He always talked about, and still talked about, is not going to be the physical land of Israel or a political arena.

I leaned in closer, curious to know how Jesus was going to answer this one.

"It's not for you to know the times and seasons that the Father has set by His authority. But you will receive power, the Holy Spirit coming upon you. You will all be my witnesses starting first in Jerusalem, then in all Judea, and then to Samaria, and even to the last part of the earth."

Just as He finished speaking the last word, He rose off the ground and floated higher and higher into the sky. We all craned our necks and shielded our eyes to watch Him ascend into the heavens, until a cloud finally hid Him from our sight.

We were still looking in amazement, wondering if He would ever come back, when suddenly two angels in white appeared beside our group.

"Men of Galilee, why do you stand looking into the sky?" they asked.

I thought it was fairly obvious. We were watching Jesus leave this earth supernaturally and waiting for further instructions.

They continued, "This same Jesus, who has been raised from you into Heaven, will come back in the same way you have seen Him go."

Then the angels just disappeared. We stood looking at each other for a few moments, then James took the lead again and said, "We should go back to Jerusalem and wait for the Holy Spirit, like Jesus said."

So we all made our way, most of us slowly in small groups, very thoughtful and quiet.

"Will the Holy Spirit be just as good as having Jesus again?" I didn't realize I had spoken aloud, so engrossed in my thoughts was I.

But Simon the Zealot, who along with his brother James, and Thomas, were walking close to me, answered, "Oh, you weren't here right after the Last Supper, were you?"

I bowed my head in shame again.

Simon patted me on the back. "I'm sorry, brother, I did not mean to bring back the condemnation. I was merely remembering that there are a few things Jesus said that you haven't heard yet. He talked a lot about the Holy Spirit that night.

"He said that if anyone loves Him, they'll keep His words, and the Father will love them. His words were His Father's, and He had spoken them to us while He was still with us. But then He spoke of sending the Holy Spirit to us to help us. He called Him the Helper. He said He would teach us all things and bring everything Jesus had taught us to our remembrance. Then He said, 'Peace I leave with you, I give my peace to you. Not as the world gives. Let not your hearts be troubled or afraid. I am going away to prepare rooms in my Father's house for you. I do as the Father has commanded me so that the world will know that I love the Father.'"

Simon sighed. "I've probably left out a lot. I don't remember everything. Hopefully, some of the others will remember other parts. Thomas, do you remember anything else?"

"I do remember that He said, 'If you loved me, you would rejoice because I said I am going to the Father, because the Father is greater than I am.' He also said something about telling us all these things to keep us from falling away. He told us that the Jews would put us out of the synagogues. He even said, 'Indeed, the hour is coming that whoever kills you will think he's doing a service to God.' But He also said that He was telling us these things so that we will remember that He prophesied to us before it happened."

James the son of Alphaeus added, "And He also said that it's advantageous to us that He go away, because if He didn't go, the Helper couldn't come to us. He told us that the Holy Spirit would convict the world of sin, righteousness, and judgment when He comes. He said He had many more things to say to us, but we couldn't handle them yet. But when the 'Spirit of truth comes, He will guide' us into truth. He won't speak on His own authority but on Jesus' authority. He will take Jesus' words and declare it to us."

This gave me a lot more to think about. Maybe the Holy Spirit would actually be better than having Jesus with us, even though I couldn't really fathom how.

When we returned to the Upper Room, all Twelve of us joined together in prayer, along with the Mary's and other women, and also, a big surprise to me, Jesus' brothers. After seeing His crucifixion and now His resurrection, they became believers just like the rest of us.

It struck me that those who had grown up with Him, had been given the greatest opportunity to believe, and only now chose to trust in Him. I guess it's never too late for anyone.

I'm living proof of that, too.

CHAPTER 32 THE REUNION AT PENTECOST

We remained in the Upper Room and waited for this Holy Spirit. We fasted and prayed often.

A few days after the Ascension, I was praying in a corner of the Upper Room. A light knock interrupted not only my prayers but all the disciples' conversations.

Silence reigned as hearts beat in the fear that we had been discovered at last.

Peter approached the door and called, "Who is it?"

"It's a messenger for Judas Iscariot from Brutus. It's about his mother."

I recognized the muffled voice as the same messenger boy. When Peter looked back at me, I nodded my permission. He cracked the door, probably to make sure the Romans or the Pharisees hadn't used him as a decoy.

When he saw that the boy was alone, he opened the door wider and motioned for him to come in.

The boy trudged in, shoulders slumped and clothes dusty. He hefted a lumpy burlap sack over his shoulders and looked around. When he saw me in the corner, he straightened and walked over.

"There ya are. Do you have any idea how hard it was for me to find this place? No one knew where you are. Lucky I got in good with a servant who works for the owner of this place. Anyway, down to business, mister. I've got another message from Brutus."

I nodded for him to continue. Considering how chatty he seemed, I was surprised he hadn't already spilled his news.

He seemed to ignore the nod, setting down the sack and reaching in to pull another date out and begin munching.

"You Southern Israelites sure have yummy fruit. These dates are the best I've ever had! Taste like honey."

I waited for him to finish chewing that date and then prodded, "Okay, what's the message?"

He wiped his mouth with the back of his hand and grinned at me. He was enjoying stringing out the suspense. Maybe it was one of the few things he could control in his life, along with which foods he bought with Brutus' money.

I determined that I wouldn't give him any more satisfaction. I wouldn't let him get a rise out of me. Besides, the poor lad was on his own without a mother or anyone to protect him. I could be patient enough to indulge his sense of drama.

I arched an eyebrow but remained silent.

After the boy ate two more dates, he cocked his head and asked, "Aren't ya dying to know what happened to your mother?"

I counted to ten in my head and then replied, "Sure. But it's up to you how to share the news. I'll let you do what you do best."

His disappointment made me chuckle inwardly.

"Fine, mister. My news is about your mother's freedom. Lucky for you, someone else was able to pay for her to go free. Wanna know who it was?"

He sure was milking this. And I really did want to know. But I took a deep breath and shrugged my shoulders. "I wouldn't mind if you told me."

"Well..." and he popped yet another date into his mouth. Once he swallowed and wiped his mouth again, he continued. "Brutus almost gave up trying to find someone else to help your mother, but then someone came to visit and paid the whole thing. It was someone you know. Can you guess?"

Boy, he was good! I almost got riled up to ask "who," but then I decided to play along.

"Let's see." I stroked my beard. "Was it the High Priest?"

The boy scoffed. "Yeah, right. Good one, mister. Try again."

"How about...Herod?"

"Okay, now you're just pulling my leg. C'mon! Give me a real guess! Last try!"

I hid my smile behind my hand. I tapped my finger to my lips. "Hmm. You're right. It's someone I know. I don't know very many people who know where my mother is. Was it...Jesus?"

He pulled back and exclaimed, "Jesus? Are you crazy? He died. I saw him!"

"I know, but He really did raise from the dead. I saw Him. I touched Him. I watched Him eat."

"Well, you're completely wrong. It was your father."

I couldn't have been more shocked if he said it was Caesar himself. "Father?"

He nodded vigorously. The gleam in his eye told me that he enjoyed seeing my discomfort. "Yep! So it seems that your mother wrote to him. He sold a bunch of stuff to be able to pay for her freedom. They were getting ready to leave together and go back to your father's house when Brutus sent me to find you. Your mother had asked him to."

I was overcome with gratitude and wonder. What could Father have possibly sold to make thirty pieces of silver? Had he gambled and gotten lucky for once, or had he changed his ways and reformed? Surely this was an answer to my prayers. I may not have been able to take care of Mother. But Adonai had.

"Praise Adonai! Thank You, Jesus!" I didn't care what anyone in that room thought of me.

Many of the disciples glanced at me, and a few began to smile, especially James and John. The boy raised his eyebrows and leaned away from me.

I wiped a tear of joy from my eye and leaned in closer to him. "Can you take a message to them for me before you go back to Brutus? Or would that put you in trouble with your master?"

He shrugged. "Sure. Brutus said I was to do anything you asked before going back. Brutus also said that he would pay me for it, but I'm sure I'll need money for supplies before I get back."

I recognized the sly look of a trickster, but I was more than willing to take care of this lad with the wonderful news.

"I don't have a lot of money, but I'll give you a little to tide you over. Wouldn't want you to faint with hunger on your way to see my mother and father, now, would we?" I reached into my pouch and pulled out the few coins I had left. I dropped them one by one into his hand.

"Okay, give them this message: Jesus has raised from the dead, and though I'm in hiding at the moment, He told us disciples to remain in Jerusalem until He sent the Holy Spirit. Ask them to come and find me. Tell them where I am—but only them, you hear?"

Though the boy nodded in agreement, I didn't trust him. He would be an easy target for the Pharisees to bribe.

"I mean it, boy. Your master would be upset with you if I—or any of us here—were to be arrested because you snitched. Okay? Can you keep your mouth shut?"

He nodded again. He seemed sincere. Hopefully fear and respect of his master would ensure his silence.

But no matter what happened, I knew that my mother and father were safe, and that was all that mattered. Adonai would continue to take care of them.

I surprised myself that I actually felt concern for my father's safety. Maybe I could forgive him like Jesus forgave me after all.

Fifty days after the Resurrection, ten days after Jesus' Ascension into Heaven, we Twelve had gathered with all the other disciples in one big house near the Temple.

We were praying and worshiping during the Feast of Weeks, the time when we gave thanks for the harvest, when suddenly there came from above a sound like a loud gust of wind, and it filled the entire house.

Over each of us, visions of forked tongues of fire hovered. We were all filled with the Holy Spirit then, and we began to "speak in tongues." That's what we called it when there was a miracle with our speech.

I could feel Him inside me, and when He spoke to my heart, it sounded like Jesus' voice but without sound. It was His words, His way of speaking, His authority, His compassion.

My heart, my mind, my body—all were in submission to the awakening of my spirit to His Spirit. It was incredible.

Many people, devout Jews living in Jerusalem, as well as many traveling pilgrims still there for the feast, heard the loud noise of the wind and came running to see what was happening. They gathered around the house and out into the street.

We continued praying and speaking, but they all heard us in their languages. However, we were all still speaking in Hebrew. At least, I think that's what happened. We spoke in Hebrew, the only language we knew, but the people heard it in their own native language.

So you might say it was more a miracle of the ear than the tongue. But regardless of how it happened, it happened, and they all understood us.

And everyone was amazed, wondering, "Aren't these all unlearned Galileans? How do we hear all of our native languages? How do we all hear them telling of the mighty works of God?"

But there were some people who mocked us, saying we were drunk.

The experience of having the Holy Spirit in me for the first time was so overwhelming, I didn't care what anyone said of me. I would have been fearful of what people thought of me before. But now, it didn't matter to me at all.

The Holy Spirit told Peter, though, to not only defend our reputation but also to share our faith with all these Jews and proselytes and travelers.

Peter stood up and addressed the crowd. "Those who live in Jerusalem, and those traveling from elsewhere, listen carefully to my words. These people are not drunk as you assume. After all, it's only morning. But the prophet Joel foretold that in the last days, God will pour out His Spirit on your sons and your daughters and your young men and your old men.' And it shall come to pass that everyone who calls upon the name of the Lord shall be saved.' You are seeing the fulfillment of that prophecy today."

He looked around. Everyone, even the hecklers, listened. He continued.

"Jesus of Nazareth—proven to be from God by His mighty deeds and the wonders that God did through Him, right here among you in Jerusalem—this Jesus was delivered up to fulfill the plan of God by being crucified. God then conquered death by raising Jesus up, because it wasn't possible for Him to be held in death's grip.

"For King David prophesied of this in the Psalms when he said that 'the Holy One would not see corruption.' We all here are eye-witnesses to Jesus' resurrection. Now that He is exalted at the right hand of God, in the place of honor in Heaven, He has now poured out that promised Holy Spirit upon us. This is what you are seeing and hearing. We are not drunk or crazy. We are blessed with a supernatural seal.

"Let all the nation of Israel therefore know without a doubt that God has made Jesus Christ both Lord and Christ—this Jesus whom you crucified."

If I hadn't been so overwhelmed with the power and joy from the presence of the Holy Spirit, I might have feared the crowd's anger against Peter when he pointed the finger at them and accused them of crucifying our Lord.

But they had cried, "Crucify him!" and said, "Let his blood be on our hands and our children's hands!"

When this assembled crowd heard his accusation, they didn't get angry, though. They didn't become a mob and thirst for violence. No, when they heard this, they recognized the truth and were cut deep to the heart.

I saw a man and a woman pushing through the crowd, calling out, but I couldn't hear them. I recognized their faces first. It was Mother and Father, and they were together! I couldn't understand what they were saying until they got almost to the back of the room where we were.

"Judas, Judas! Son! We're here!"

"Mother! You're safe! You're free!" I wrapped my arms around her in a big bear hug. "Thank you, Lord Jesus! This day is complete."

But the Spirit pricked my heart. No, there is still more to come.

What could possibly be better than receiving the Holy Spirit and my Mother in one day?

I pulled back to look into Mother's tear-stained but glowing face. She put her hand on my cheek and patted it gently. Then she glanced over her shoulder. Father. Could forgiveness be possible on top of the miracles already occurring today?

I nodded at him. "Father? Thank you for freeing Mother when I couldn't pay for it."

He nodded and rubbed his hand across the back of his neck.

"I...I'm sorry, Son. For everything. I got rid of all my wine. I sold everything I could to pay for your Mother's freedom. I hope...that it makes up for a little of my sins over the years."

My eyes filled with tears. A close relationship with him might still take a while to work through all the hurt feelings, but such a promising start as this was nothing short of miraculous.

"Yes, Father. I'm also sorry for blaming you all these years for every bad thing in my life. Will you forgive me, too?"

I had not seen that soft look in his eyes since that fateful day of Mother's captivity. He stuck his hand out, and I reached out mine to shake it. He clapped his other hand on my back.

There we were. A whole family again. I had never allowed myself to imagine it.

Meanwhile, many in the crowd began calling out to Peter, "What should we do?"

Peter, exultation beaming from his plain face, now acted like a charismatic leader. He smiled and answered, "Repent! Just repent and be baptized in the name of Jesus Christ in order to be forgiven of your sins. Then you will receive the gift of the Holy Spirit, too. For this promise is for you and for your children. It is also for all those far off. So save yourselves from this evil generation and believe."

Three thousand souls received his message gladly, including both Mother and Father. They all believed on Jesus the Christ as their Savior and Lord, repented from their old sins, and were baptized. That day was a great harvest of souls into the Eternal Kingdom of Jesus Christ. And that was just the beginning.

I have pledged my life to spread the Good News of Jesus' death and resurrection to all Jews and even to the Gentiles now. I remember how Jesus' last words on earth to us were, "Go and make disciples..."

Father, Mother, and I are all making disciples together. This is the greatest mission ever.

Now you go and fulfill Jesus' Great Commission, too.

THE END

ENDNOTES: BIBLE REFERENCES

*Much of the timeline for Biblical events comes from *Baker's Harmony of the Gospels* (King James Version) by Benjamin Davies, Editor (Grand Rapids, MI: Baker Book House, 1994).

*Chapter 1 the Calling: Luke 5:27-29 Capernaum; Mark 2:13-14 Levi, son of Alphaeus, Capernaum; Matt. 9:9 tax booth in Jesus' own city; Jewish use of Adonai instead of Yahweh: "the Names of God" by Lavinia Cohn-Sherbok at https://www.myjewishlearning.com/article/the-names-of-god/

*Chapter 2 the Wedding: Matthew 11:2-6; Matt. 4:13-16; Luke 4:16-31; John 2:1-12; 7:2-10

*Chapter 3 the Chosen: Luke 6:12-16; Matt. 10:2-4; Mark 3:16-19

*Chapter 4 the Mount: Luke 6:6-49; Matt. 5-7

*Chapter 5 the Cost: Luke 14:25-35, Luke 16:1-13; John 10:11; Matt. 11:2-6; 15:21-28

*Chapter 6 the Trip: The MacMillan Bible Atlas, Yohanah Aharoni and Michael Avi-Yonah, 1993, p.173; "Ptolemais" at Bible Study Tools, https://www.biblestudytools.com/dictionary/ptolemais/

*Chapter 7 the Feeding: Matt. 14:13-21; Luke 9:11-17; Deut. 18:15-18; John 1:21-26; John 7:41-43

*Chapter 8 the Storm: Matt. 14:22-33; Mark 4:35-41; John 6:22-71

*Chapter 9 the Meeting: none

*Chapter 10 the Transfiguration: Mark 9:2-29; Luke 9:28-43; Matthew 17:1-20

*Chapter 11 the Greatest: Mark 9:33-37, 10:1-9; Matt. 18:1-10, 19:1-15

*Chapter 12 the Sinners: Luke 19:1-10; Matt. 8:5-13; Luke 7:1-10; Matt. 15:21-28

*Chapter 13 the Declaration: John 1:21, 25; 7:40; Duet. 18:18; Matt. 16:13-21; Mark 8:27-30, 31-38

*Chapter 14 the Resurrection & the Life: Matt. 16:21, 24-28, 17:22-23; 20:17-19; Mark 8:31-38, 10:32-34; John 11:1-53; http://www.ntgreek.net/lesson23.htm

*Chapter 15 the Entry: Zechariah 9:9-13; Matthew 21:1-11; Mark 11:1-11; Luke 19:28-40; John 12:12-19

*Chapter 16 the Anointing: John 12:1-11; Matt. 26:6-13; Mark 14:1-9

*Chapter 17 the Cleansing: Matt 21:12-17; Mark 11:15-19, 27-33

*Chapter 18 the Plan: Matt 26:14-16; Mark 14:10-11; Luke 22:1-6; https://en.wikipedia.org/wiki/Hall_of_Hewn_Stones

*Chapter 19 the Servant: John 13:1-17

*Chapter 20 the Warning: Matt 26:20-25; Mark 14:17-20; Luke 22:20-23; John 13:18-30; Luke 11:17; Matt. 12:25; Exodus 12:5-11, ESV; Matt. 26:25, NLT.

*Chapter 21 the War Within: Acts 1:18-19; Matt. 27:3-10; 2 Cor. 7:9-10

*Chapter 22 Forgiveness: John 18:1-12

*Chapter 23 the Abandon: Matt. 26:30-35, 47-57; Mark 14:26-31, 43-53; http://www.yaiy.org/questions/answers/names12.html; John 6:35, 14:6, 8:12, 10:11-18; 10:7-10, 11:25, 18:5-6; Psalm 23:1-6

*Chapter 24 the Crucifixion: Mark 14:66-15:1-47; John 19:1-42; Matt. 27:11-56

*Chapter 25 \the Death of Hopes: Mark 15:46

*Chapter 26 the Doubters: Matthew 28:1-15; Mark 16:1-13; Luke 24:1-45; John 20:1-29; Luke 7:11-17; 8:41-42, 49-53

*Chapter 27 the Emmaus Road: Matthew 28:11-15; Luke 24:13-35; John 20:19-25

*Chapter 28 the Impossible: Mark 16:14-20: Matt. 28:16-20; Luke 24:46-49; Mark 9:24

*Chapter 29 the Breakfast: John 21:1-25

*Chapter 30 the Messenger: none

*Chapter 31 the Commission: Acts 1:2-14; John 14:23-31; 16:1-15

*Chapter 32 the Reunion at Pentecost: Acts 2:1-41; https://en.m.wikipedia.org/wiki/Shavuot

LIST OF RESOURCES

B*enefit of the Doubt* by Gregory A. Boyd
    "Did Judas Have Free Will" by Dave Jenkins at Christianity.com

ACKNOWLEDGMENTS:

We thank the Lord for everything, not limited to saving our souls, bringing us together, and giving us the inspiration for this story of redemption.

Thank you to our beta readers and editors, including Sally Shupe, Gayle Long, and Robert Kugler.

Thanks especially to Kate Johnson, writing coach, for her insightful and encouraging big-picture analysis! To see her offered services, visit her at https://katejohnstonauthor.com/writing-and-editing-services/.

THANK YOU!

✱If you liked this imaginative, speculative Biblical fiction about Judas Iscariot, would you just take a couple minutes to write a short, honest review? It can be just a sentence or two. It not only helps authors more than you may realize, but it also helps other readers know what to expect out of this book. Thank you!

ABOUT THE AUTHORS

Lila was born in 1978 and grew up in the tiny farming community of Notus, Idaho. Chris was born in 1979, grew up in Texas, and moved to North Carolina at the age of 11. He met Lila at the Christian college they graduated from, married her in 2002, and brought her back to NC.

They have two energetic boys ages 15 and 11, a hyper dachshund Brownie, and a silly cat Callie. Growing up in church, both Chris and Lila accepted the Lord at young ages and graduated from a Bible college, Lila with a 4-year Humanities degree and Chris with a 4-year Mathematics degree. Lila has published four Christian Romance novels, the "Love is..." series based on 1 Corinthians 13, the Love Chapter. Chris has published a nonfiction book on studying the Bible.

When not homeschooling their boys or writing, you can find them studying the Bible, binge-watching shows, playing video games, creating art (Lila only), or playing chess and Pokemon (Chris only).

Connect with Lila at liladiller.com to learn how to show *agape* love to others and draw closer to Jesus through both fiction and Bible study.

Connect also on social media by following Lila on:

Facebook – facebook.com/loveisseries

Twitter – twitter.com/DillerLila

Instagram – instagram.com/liladiller

OTHER BOOKS BY LILA DILLER:

The contemporary Christian romance "Love is..." series (These are all ebook links. To find links to print and audiobook links, go to liladiller.com/books):

1. *Her Heart's Decision* – you can download it for free when you sign up for Lila's email list at www.liladiller.com/landingpagefor1

2. *Her Heart's Jealousy*

3. *Her Heart's Impatience*

4. *Her Heart's Disappointment*

Lightning Source UK Ltd.
Milton Keynes UK
UKHW010633010422
400950UK00001B/83